No Time For Love

"Hi, Gary," Nancy said to the *Wilder Times* photographer. "Do you want to sign up for the Ten-K race?"

"Me? Have no fear," Gary replied. He whipped his arm from behind his back and handed Nancy a bouquet of flowers exploding with purples and reds and yellows and lots of white baby's breath.

"For me?" Nancy choked. "Uh, thanks, Gary, but what's the occasion?" Then she saw that her name on the little envelope was written in Jake's handwriting and tore it open.

Hey, Miss Reporter—you're pretty AND smart!
Congratulations! Call me . . . Jake

"These are so sweet," Nancy said, burying her nose in the blooms and inhaling deeply. "But couldn't he deliver them in person?" Gary just shrugged.

The problem was that Nancy wanted to give Jake a huge hug. She'd been waiting to give him the news of her promotion face-to-face and to revel in his congratulatory kisses. Gary wouldn't do as a substitute.

I guess Jake's just too busy, Nancy thought.

Nancy Drew on Campus™

Available from ARCHWAY Paperbacks

Nancy Drew
on campus ™ #7

False
Friends

Carolyn Keene

AN ARCHWAY PAPERBACK

Published by POCKET BOOKS
New York London Toronto Sydney Tokyo Singapore

This book is a work of fiction. Names, characters, places and incidents are products of the author's imagination or are used fictiously. Any resemblance to actual events or locales or persons, living or dead, is entirely coincidental.

AN ARCHWAY PAPERBACK *Original*

An Archway Paperback published by
POCKET BOOKS, a division of Simon & Schuster Inc.
1230 Avenue of the Americas, New York, NY 10020

Copyright © 1996 by Simon & Schuster Inc.
Produced by Mega-Books, Inc.

ISBN: 0-671-52751-7

First Archway Paperback printing March 1996

10 9 8 7 6 5 4 3 2 1

NANCY DREW, AN ARCHWAY PAPERBACK and colophon are registered trademarks of Simon & Schuster Inc.

NANCY DREW ON CAMPUS is a trademark of Simon & Schuster Inc.

Cover photos by Pat Hill Studio

Printed in the U.S.A.

IL 8+

CHAPTER 1

This is better than my wildest dreams," George Fayne excitedly whispered to herself as she surveyed the scene around her. Nancy should really be here to see this, she thought, referring to her close friend, Nancy Drew.

Pushing up the sleeves of her baggy gray Earthworks sweatshirt, George smiled at the lively chaos before her.

The wide, sun-drenched steps in front of Wilder University's Student Union were filled with students in colorful running gear enjoying the mild weather. A huge, rainbow-striped banner flapped in the warm breeze between the arches.

10K ROAD RACE, THIS SUNDAY!
Cosponsored by Earthworks, Pi Phi, and
W.U. Track & Field
Prerace pasta dinner Saturday nite!
Postrace bash at Pi Phi with live DJ!
REGISTER HERE!

1

Everyone was buzzing excitedly about the race, lining up behind men's and women's registration tables, adding their names to the growing lists of participants. Race numbers and Earthworks T-shirts were stacked on the tables.

"Awesome job, you organization queen," a familiar voice buzzed in her ear.

George whirled around and hugged her handsome boyfriend, Will Blackfeather. "I hope I see *you* out there," she said.

"Me?" Will replied in mock horror. "I was the first to sign up. But I'm going to sit this one out to help with the race. You're going to be racing, so I figure someone is needed to handle emergencies."

"But you paid your registration fee!"

Smiling, Will tightened his grip on George. "It's my donation to Earthworks."

George poked him playfully and asked him to pray for no rain on Sunday.

Will put a soothing hand on her shoulder. "You'll do fine in the race, rain or no rain," he said.

"I need to," George replied worriedly. "If I make a good qualifying time, I'll better my chances for getting a place on the track team. It'll make the coaches notice me. Now that I've given up crew, I won't have a sport if I don't make the track team."

Will became concerned. "I hope you're still glad you quit crew."

George nodded. "Totally. There's no way I can

do both crew and track and stay on top of school-work, not to mention Earthworks."

Will cleared his throat. "Ahem."

Leaning against Will's body, George breathed in his now familiar musky aroma, and a little thrill ran through her. "Yes, and pay attention to *you*," she added, smiling.

"Just checking," Will said. "Anyway, even if it rains on Sunday, you'll blow everyone away," he assured her. "You're in such great shape."

The campus clock tower chimed twelve noon, and seconds later crowds of students flooded out the doors of the classroom buildings. Classes ended early on Friday—and by twelve o'clock the weekend had unofficially begun.

The quad was packed, and more and more people joined the registration lines. Others strolled over to check the sign-up list.

"Look at all these people!" someone called giddily to George.

Kara Verbeck, Nancy Drew's roommate, saun-tered over, a denim hat pulled down over her sun-streaked brown hair.

"Thanks for offering to help out today," George said. "Ready to work at a registration table?"

Kara was scanning the men's line. "Am I ever," she said brightly. "But only if I get *that* table."

"I saved it just for you." George laughed.

George noticed Will's eyes glued to the spot where Stephanie Keats, another one of Nancy's suitemates, was leaning against a lamppost. Sleek and hard-bodied, with long, black tousled hair and perfectly manicured nails, she was wearing black Lycra running shorts and a pink jogging bra.

"Hey, put your eyes back in your head," she kidded, giving Will a playful slap.

Will reddened. "It's amazing what a fashion show racing and even registration have become," he said, trying to cover himself.

George laughed. "Nice try."

Kara clucked her tongue. "No harm in looking," she said dreamily. Zeroing in on a slim, shirtless guy who was filling out his forms, she sighed. "I guess it's time for me to get to work."

She sure is in good shape, George thought, looking at Stephanie, for someone whose only exercise is the cigarette-to-the-mouth lift. "Hey, Stephanie!" she called out. "I didn't know you were a runner."

Stephanie arched a perfectly plucked eyebrow. "Runner?" she called back, as though running were the last thing on her mind. "I was just passing by."

Laughing, George stepped over to the men's table to see how Kara was doing.

"George, you remember Montana Smith," Kara said, indicating the skinny girl with corkscrew blond curls working next to her. "She's pledging Pi Phi, too."

"Sure, you were one of the leaders of the Kappa protest," George said, referring to a Pi Phi pledge prank that Montana and some of her fellow pledges had done at a Kappa party. "Hi, Montana."

But Montana was busy staring at an incredibly muscular young man in line.

"The registration fee is ten dollars?" George heard the guy asking Montana.

Montana blinked, her mouth frozen in a grin. Kara just shrugged.

George stepped in, all cheer. "Yeah, and you get a lot for it," she explained. "A prerace pasta dinner with the best spaghetti sauce in town, a postrace dance at Pi Phi with the best local DJ. *Plus* you get to support Earthworks and the track and field team. It's definitely the best investment of ten dollars you'll make this year."

Everyone around the table was nodding.

"What does Earthworks do?" the guy asked.

George stepped back, curious about what Montana would say.

Montana opened her mouth, but all she managed to say was "Uh—"

"Well," Kara tried to help, waving her pencil. "It, um, helps clean the air, and—"

"Recycles," George whispered.

"Recycles!" Montana blurted out.

The guy cocked his head. "Aren't you guys supposed to be the *environmental* sorority?"

"So?" Montana asked.

"So you're supposed to know all this stuff," he said. "You *are* sponsoring the race, aren't you?"

George was ready to jump in and bail them out, but she was kind of enjoying their struggle.

Kara nudged Montana. "Why don't you just

put your phone number right next to your name, and we'll get back to you with all the information you want. In fact, here's my number—call me anytime."

"But what about Tim?" George cried as the guy walked away shaking his head.

"I haven't forgotten Tim," Kara replied, acting shocked. "Tim is wonderful. I'm just being nice, you know, to get everyone to sign up."

"Yeah, whatever." Montana sniffed. "But you already have a boyfriend, so let me give out *my* phone number. *I'm* the one who needs a date."

Rolling her eyes, George patted their shoulders. "Looks like you two have things under control," she said. "Keep it up."

Montana was already smiling up at the next guy, nudging Kara out of the way.

"You can count on us," Kara said, holding her ground and offering the guy a sign-up sheet and pencil.

Nancy Drew was in a great mood as she hustled across the campus quad. With her books hugged to her chest, and her strawberry blond hair blowing in the warm breeze, she smiled at just about everyone she passed.

Taking a bite of a candy bar, Nancy was happy to think of nothing but the long weekend stretching ahead of her. She was in a festive mood and was psyched about the race, and about everything in general. Mostly, though, she was psyched about Jake Collins.

I still can't believe it's me, Nancy giddily thought to herself as she replayed their last kiss.

The fact was, until a couple weeks ago she'd only known Jake as the star reporter for the campus newspaper, *Wilder Times,* where Nancy was a freshman reporter. She'd seen him at editorial meetings, but they hadn't been friends.

I never believed I'd get close to him, Nancy thought to herself as she crossed the quad. He was kind of intimidating because of his style and looks: his signature steel-tipped black cowboy boots, wavy brown hair, and deep brown eyes that met everyone's gaze steadily.

But now he was more to Nancy than just a dedicated reporter with an incredibly sexy aura.

Now he's my boyfriend! Nancy felt like screaming out.

Nancy spotted George on the steps of the Student Union, pointing and waving as she shouted out instructions to both volunteers and runners.

"If you were wearing a uniform, you'd look like a traffic cop," Nancy said as she sidled up to her friend.

George laughed. "I feel like one."

Nancy observed the scene and spoke with admiration to her friend. "I've got to hand it to you and the other volunteers, George, it's a success already, and you haven't even fired the starting gun."

George was shaking her head. "That Montana is such a space cadet! Listen to her."

Nancy followed George over to the men's registration table.

"It doesn't matter if you're a runner or not, enter the race because of the cool party afterward." Montana was convincing a serious-looking young man. "After all, *I'll* be there."

Nancy and George broke up.

"You can't lose," George assured the guy.

Montana pointed at the paper. "Now put your name right there."

George rolled her eyes as she led Nancy away. "Nothing like an event to bring the goofballs out of the woodwork," she confided. "You should have seen Stephanie hanging out in her 'running clothes.' " George shuddered.

Nancy laughed. "Stephanie? She can't even run to the shower in the morning."

"Well, you should have seen the traffic jam of guys around her," George said.

"I'm sure she loved that," Nancy said. "Oh, by the way, I stopped by to let you know I'll set up a registration table for the race at Thayer tomorrow morning."

"Excellent! Your resident advisor got permission from the residential office?"

Nancy shook her head. "I left a note for Dawn two days ago, but I haven't seen her. I asked Bill Graham, the second-floor R.A., to okay it."

George was eyeing the snaking lines. "I never knew so many people at Wilder were runners."

Nancy shrugged. "People know a good cause when they see one. Well, I have to get going," she said excitedly. "I'm late for a meeting at the paper."

"Anybody in particular you're going to 'meet'?" George grinned.

Nancy cocked her head. *"Moi?* Actually I'm not meeting Jake today. I've been summoned to the office of our editor-in-chief, Gail. But maybe if I'm really lucky and really good I'll run into Jake."

"So what do you say, are you going to leave everyone in the dust, or what?" Tall and athletically handsome Jamal Lewis was joking with his girlfriend, Pam Miller, as they raced through the archway into the quad.

Breathing easily and evenly, Pam tucked some stray hairs from her long, black mane under her backward baseball cap. Even though she was running with Jamal, who was faster and stronger, she'd kept up. Jamal was supposed to be leading her on a relaxed warm-up for Sunday's race, but his pace quickened, and Pam wasn't the sort of runner to be left behind. She hated to lose, even to a friend. She'd found her stride early on, when they were circling the small lake on the outskirts of campus, and by the time they reached the quad, they were in an all-out sprint. But Jamal beat her by only a couple of feet.

They slowed to a jog and stopped, breathing hard, near the end of the race registration lines.

"Looking good, Miller," Jamal panted.

Pam bent over to catch her breath. "I just want a good finish time."

Jamal's eyes glinted. "Uh-huh, sure, like I believe that. You're too competitive for that, Pam.

You said yourself you hate running against the clock. You need other people to keep you from getting lazy."

Pam shrugged, raising her long, burnished arms above her head to stretch out.

"Hey, guys."

George ambled up, giving her roommate a high-five. "You ready for the race?"

Jamal laughed. "Pam told me she was going to leave you in the dust."

"Jamal!" Pam turned imploringly to George. "I did not!"

"That's okay," George said, grinning. "Because if you don't, that's where I'll leave you."

Jamal stepped between them and mimicked a referee breaking up a fight. "Okay, girls. Both of you back to your corners."

Pam playfully slapped Jamal's hand away. "George, you'll be so distracted with your Earthworks stuff that you won't be able to concentrate on running."

"Okay, let's cool it!" George complained. "Do I have to keep telling you about what an excellent organization Earthworks is—"

"Yeah, for those of you who eat veggie burgers and fight to save the northwest African butterswallow," Jamal wisecracked.

George and Pam looked at each other. *"Butterswallow?"* they said in unison.

Jamal shrugged. "Yeah. The butterswallow. You know—"

"All right." George sighed. "Once and for all I'm going to tell you what Earthworks does."

Counting off on her fingers, she outlined all the great environmental projects Earthworks was involved in.

Out of the corner of her eye, Pam could see Jamal nodding. She was really proud of George. In just a few weeks, George had managed to get herself involved in all sides of Wilder life. "You definitely deserve all the help you can get," Pam said.

Jamal reached into the little hideaway pocket of his runner's shorts. "Totally," he said, and brought out a sweat-dampened ten-dollar bill. "Here's ten dollars. It's all I have on me."

"Excellent, Jamal," George said. "That's really generous. Then you'll run, too?"

Jamal waved her off. "Nah. I'll leave that high-speed chase stuff to you two. It's going to be smokin' out there. Just use the money however you need it."

Pam propped herself up against Jamal's back to stretch her lean legs. She could feel George eyeing her.

"You're really in great shape," George said.

Pam smiled. "You, too. Sunday's going to be fun."

"Fun," George repeated contemplatively. "I guess—as long as I get in a good time."

"You? No sweat. Just make sure you load up on carbs at the pasta dinner."

George's eyes flashed, and she poked her roommate. "You too, you know. You're going to need it if you're going to keep up with me."

Pam cocked her head. "Oh, really? Just watch

yourself in bed. You never know what strange accidents might befall you in the middle of the night!"

As Nancy was cutting across the quad toward the *Wilder Times* offices, she passed a table set up in front of Graves Hall. Two girls she'd seen in some of her classes were sitting in chairs, chatting with friends. A guy she didn't recognize was handing out pamphlets. A modest but tastefully printed sign hung from the table's edge: REACH—Support, Understanding, Peace.

"Hey, you have a second?"

Nancy raised her head. One of the girls behind the table had called out to her. She had a warm, agreeable smile, pretty blond hair, and wide, friendly eyes.

"Not really," Nancy said apologetically. "I have an appointment—"

"No problem," the girl said. "Maybe next time."

"But what's your group about?" Nancy asked quickly.

"Basically, it's a support group," the girl replied. "We study together, and it's really great. But you're in a rush. We'll talk later."

The guy with the pamphlets lifted his hand in a cordial wave. "We'll be here."

Hmm, Nancy thought to herself as she headed for the newspaper building. I guess there are probably kids who need that kind of support. But who has any free time anyway?

Just then Nancy's hand was grabbed, and she

felt herself being whisked off the path and into the cavelike coolness under a giant weeping willow.

"One word from you, and I'll, I'll—"

"You'll do what, Jake Collins," Nancy replied dryly.

"I'll—"

Nancy felt a soft, still slightly unfamiliar mouth press against hers.

"Do that," Jake said.

"Ooh," Nancy replied, a sheepish grin tugging at the corners of her mouth.

She raised her ocean blue eyes and let them wander over Jake's boyishly handsome face, settling on his warm lips that seemed frozen in a wry, I-know-something-you-don't grin.

Nancy wanted to pinch herself. Is this really me? she wondered.

"Okay," Jake said, releasing Nancy's hand. "No time for fun and games. I have places to go, things to do—"

"People to see," Nancy finished the expression.

Jake poked her in the forehead. "That's right. People to see! You'd better get going. Come on. No time to chitchat."

He grabbed her hand and led her back into the sunshine toward the *Wilder Times* office.

"Oh, there's Steve," Jake said, motioning to the opening door.

The man at the door waved. Nancy didn't know Professor Shapiro very well. She did know he was the faculty advisor for the newspaper and one of Jake's friends.

Catching Jake pointing at the top of her head, Nancy turned to Professor Shapiro in time to see him giving Jake the okay sign before he took off across the quad.

"What are you doing?" Nancy asked, laughing.

"Oh, nothing," Jake said elusively.

Nancy peered at him. "Come on! Tell me what's going on?"

"You want to be the investigative reporter. I guess you'll have to figure it out yourself," Jake teased, and set off down the path.

"He can be such a flake sometimes," Nancy said to herself as she took the stairs up to the newspaper's office.

Inside, she headed for a door that said Gail Gardeski, Editor-in-Chief.

"Hi, Gail. Sorry I'm late. Jake corralled me outside—"

Gail flashed Nancy a warm smile.

That's weird, Nancy thought. Gail almost never smiles at me.

Gail was wearing a sun-bleached blue polo shirt over a linen skirt, and a string of African beads. She was small and thin, with a long, Roman nose and big green eyes, and though she was only a college senior Nancy thought she already had the serious, short-tempered manner of an editor at a big-time newspaper.

"I asked you to come in here today," Gail began, "because I've been talking with Steve Shapiro, our faculty advisor."

Nancy swallowed. If Gail wasn't smiling, she'd

swear she was about to be given the ax. "I just saw him outside," Nancy said.

Gail raised an eyebrow. "Then he told you?"

Nancy cocked her head. "Told me—?"

"That you've been promoted?"

Nancy almost shouted. "Promoted!"

"Yes," Gail replied matter-of-factly. "Congratulations. You're a full reporter."

Nancy blushed. This was the very thing she'd been waiting for from the first day she'd started working on the paper!

Stay calm, she commanded herself. *Calm.*

"Wow," she sputtered, "I mean, *really.* I mean, that's great."

Gail smiled again—twice in the same meeting, Nancy thought, dumbfounded.

"This is the fastest we've ever promoted a cub reporter," Gail said, nodding. "But everyone on the editorial board thought you deserved a chance."

"But has Professor Shapiro read anything I've written?"

"I assume so," Gail replied. "But it's not really his decision. And *I've* read all your work."

"Of course you have," Nancy said quickly. "I didn't mean anything by that." Nancy could hardly keep her thoughts straight. Her brain was swimming with new story ideas already!

"So," Gail went on, "you'll still get regular staff assignments, but now you can suggest stories you'd like to follow. I'll try to approve at least one feature article for you a month. It's a lot of work. Can you handle it?"

Nancy nodded firmly. "I can, and I will—"

Gail held up her hand. "The decision has been made by the board. But before it's officially announced to the rest of the staff, Professor Shapiro would like to talk to you personally. How's tomorrow?"

Nancy nodded. "Tomorrow's great." She hopped to her feet and started out of the office. Then she stopped herself and turned around. "Thanks, Gail."

"You deserve it," Gail said, getting back to work.

Nancy was off, down the stairs, and out into the sunshine. Then she remembered Jake's antics. Obviously, he knew about this.

Nancy looked up and down the path, eyeing the trees, wondering if Jake was lurking there, waiting for her. But how did he know about her promotion if Gail hadn't announced it yet?

CHAPTER 2

In satiny blue running tights and a white sweatshirt, her blond ponytail swinging, Bess Marvin and her Kappa sorority sister Holly Thornton strolled up to the race registration tables.

"Bess!" George said, steering her cousin over to the women's table. "Just in time."

Don't let me catch my breath or anything, Bess thought to herself as George pressed a box of pens and a stack of registration forms into her hands.

"Do you know Montana, Bess?" Kara called over from the men's table, nodding to the girl next to her.

Montana wrinkled her nose in fake disgust. "We've met."

"Yes," Bess said, "I believe you were holding a picket sign?"

"Hey, what are you guys doing here anyway?" Kara asked. "I thought this was a Pi Phi thing."

"It's not *just* a Pi Phi event," Holly replied dryly. "The Kappas have always thought that Earthworks was worthwhile even if we have to endure a few stray Pi Phis."

"All right, girls," George said, stepping between the tables. "Back to work. Sign those runners up."

Bess heard George whisper in her ear. "What's tall, sandy-haired, and has the whitest and straightest teeth known to mankind?"

"Are you feeling all right?" Bess inquired. "I think you've been out in the sun too long."

"The answer to my question is coming across the quad, making a beeline straight for you."

Bess looked up and swallowed hard. "Paul," she whispered as Paul Cody jogged up. No, she hadn't forgotten him. How could she after he showed such interest in her at the Kappa opening-night party for the drama department's production of *Grease!* Unfortunately, she'd forced herself to brush him off because of a promise she made to herself to spend more time with her books. If she didn't get her grades up, she wouldn't be around Wilder much longer. So that didn't leave time for men right now.

But his adorable face had been rattling around in her brain since the party, gnawing at her like a great opportunity thrown away.

"Hi," he said, pulling up next to the registration table. "Remember me?"

"Paul, right?" Bess said.

Paul smiled, revealing those perfect pearly whites, which were set off even more by his tan. Bess thought he looked wonderful.

"You remember," he said.

"Sure. Are you running in the race on Sunday?" Bess asked, eyeing his new running shoes and lean legs.

Paul shrugged. "Hadn't thought about it—"

"Think about it," Bess said earnestly. "It's for a good cause. And there's a great party afterward."

"Is the prize a date with you?" Paul asked.

Bess's jaw dropped. Great looking and quick on his feet, too, she thought.

Paul blushed. "Sorry, I shouldn't have said that. I was kidding."

"Oh," Bess replied, struggling not to show the disappointment on her face. "Run in the race anyway."

Bess's eyes locked on his. There it was again—that little flutter in her stomach.

"You're always organizing something, aren't you," Paul said.

Bess cocked her head.

"That Kappa party for *Grease!*" Paul reminded her. "It was really fun."

Bess waved him off. "Oh, that."

"And now this."

"Actually—" Bess lowered her voice to a stage whisper. "This is really a Pi Phi event, but promise you won't tell anybody."

Paul put a hand over his heart. "Your secret's safe. But I hope your hectic schedule's the only reason I'm having a hard time catching up with you."

Bess could practically feel George's stare searing the back of her head, waiting to see what she'd say. "You've been wanting to catch up with *me?*" Bess replied innocently.

Paul blushed a deeper shade of red. "Well, yeah, I wanted to know—"

"I figured it out!" Holly broke in between race applicants, waving at Paul. "I've been trying to place you. You're a Zeta, right?"

As Paul nodded, Bess's good mood evaporated. The very mention of the Zetas made her blood run cold.

Not long ago, a Zeta brother named Dave Cantera had made a more than forceful pass at her, which she'd just barely managed to escape intact. Even though she'd recovered from the horrible incident and had helped get Cantera kicked off campus for selling drugs, Bess still wasn't ready to get involved with another fraternity guy. Especially a Zeta.

I wonder if Paul was one of those jerks who wolf-whistled and tossed off lewd comments as Dave led me on his little "tour" of their house? she thought.

"So," she said coolly, "did you know Dave?"

Paul sighed. "Who didn't? I'm glad he's expelled. Giving him a chance to pledge Zeta was the biggest mistake the fraternity ever made. And I'm really glad you helped get rid of him."

Bess cocked her head. The university authorities assured Bess her involvement in Cantera's expulsion wouldn't get out. "How did you know it was me?"

Paul lowered his voice. "No secrets inside a fraternity house, didn't you know that? But don't worry. All the brothers are grateful to you. You're welcome anytime."

"I am?" Bess choked.

"Hey, I hear Zeta won the Zero Award last year for being the only frat not to support a single worthwhile thing on campus." Paul shifted back and forth on his feet. "We're trying to change all that," he said quietly. "At least, I am." Paul caught Bess's eye. "Would signing up for the race be worth a few points?"

Maybe being a Zeta isn't so terrible after all, Bess started to think.

But her thoughts were interrupted.

"Ready for some power studying, Marvin?" a familiar voice called out before Bess could answer.

Brian Daglian marched over with his book bag slung over his shoulder, his deep blue eyes fixed on her.

"I guess," Bess murmured as she got up to leave.

"Is that an 'I guess the race is worth a few points,' or an 'I guess I'm ready for power studying'?" Paul asked.

"Both," Bess replied, trying to be polite.

"What are you so down in the dumps for?" Brian asked as he dropped his book bag onto the table.

"She's distracted," Holly said.

Brian stepped in. "The only distraction Bess needs comes in the form of paper and pencil and library card," he said sternly.

"Yes, O Book-Master," Bess mumbled.

Holly grabbed her and pulled her aside. "Paul's one of the few Zetas who's really honest and nice," she whispered.

Bess nodded. "He does look honest—"

"And nice," Holly reminded her. "Look at those eyes. Let him ask you out. He wants to."

Bess looked at her. "How can you tell?"

"It's written all over his face, dummy," Holly said impatiently.

"Oh, Bess!" Brian called.

Bess sighed. "I have to go, Holly. Take it easy."

Holly was glancing back and forth between Bess and Paul, giving Bess a what-are-you-crazy? look.

"My grades," Bess explained to Paul. "They stink. See you later."

"Not if I see you first," Paul shot back. He was smiling with those incredible teeth again, but his face expressed his disappointment.

" 'Library, books,' repeat that after me," Brian instructed.

" 'Library, books,' " Bess echoed unenthusiastically, falling into step beside him.

As she and Brian waded into the crowd, Bess glanced back over her shoulder. Paul was watching her.

No, Marvin, she commanded herself. He may be trustworthy, and Zeta may not be such a house of horrors, but you don't have time for guys now. No matter how hot they are, or funny, or . . .

"Or sweet," she whispered.

By the time Nancy got back to Suite 301 in Thayer Hall, she was breathing hard. She'd been racing all over, looking for people to tell about her promotion.

Jake wasn't at his apartment, and when she went back to the registration tables, George was off running an errand and Bess had left for the library.

After slipping through the suite door, Nancy leaned against the wall, running her fingers through her hair. "That's okay," she consoled herself. But as much as she tried to be ecstatic, somehow her promotion to full-fledged reporter just didn't seem real yet. For as long as she could remember, whenever something good happened to her, the first thing she did was tell Bess and George. "Well, I guess I'll have to tell them later," she said wistfully.

In her room she sat at her desk, took out a textbook, and opened it. Then, sighing, she closed it. After kicking off her sneakers, she threw her feet onto her bed and stared out the window and felt a smile creep across her face.

"You're a full reporter now," Nancy reminded herself.

She flipped open a notebook and wrote across the top: "Good Story Ideas," and underlined it twice. Then she thought—and thought. . . .

When Nancy caught herself filling the columns with doodles, she erased them.

She thought of Jake.

"Freshmen dating upperclassmen!" she blurted out, and wrote that down. She frowned and erased it. "Too boring. Maybe a piece on the freshman experience. Like a journal."

As she thought she drummed a quick, steady rhythm on the top of her desk with the eraser of her pencil.

"No," she said. Listening to the calls of some students playing touch football under her window, she knew she wasn't going to get any homework done. And no good story ideas were coming to her, either.

Her stomach growled as she stared at her watch. "Three o'clock," she murmured. "I can't study, and I can't do work, I guess I'll have to eat."

Her eyes fell on an open bag of nacho chips on Kara's bed.

It's amazing how Kara stuffs her face with junk food all day and doesn't gain an ounce, Nancy mused.

She reached for the open bag, but it was empty.

"Food!" Nancy commanded, snapping off the light and bolting out of her room.

She headed down the hall and saw a crack of light running down one side of Dawn Steiger's door.

"Dawn? Guess what happened to me today?" Nancy called out as she knocked.

The force of the knock pushed the door open. Nancy stuck her head inside. "Why's your door—"

The room was empty. The bed was made, the pillow fluffed. The window was closed, which meant that Dawn wasn't around because Nancy knew that Dawn loved fresh air.

"Then why is her door open?" she wondered out loud.

Shrugging, Nancy turned to leave when she noticed a piece of paper under her shoe. She bent over to read it.

"Weird," Nancy said. "That's the note I slid under her door two days ago about the permission for the registration table. Guess she didn't notice it."

Nancy glanced around the room for something to write another note on. She wanted to remind Dawn to come to the prerace pasta party Saturday night. But strangely, there wasn't any paper lying around.

"It's as though she's packed up and left," Nancy murmured.

She opened a desk drawer and found a piece of paper, and began to write.

But before she got very far, she noticed deep in the drawer a copy of the *Wilder Times* from early the past week. Nancy pulled it out. An ad was circled in red, and then again in blue:

Need Love? REACH for it.
A gift of Support, Understanding & Peace
Call Mitch for meeting details, 633–7290

"REACH," Nancy repeated to herself, picturing that table she had seen on the quad earlier that day.

Shrugging, Nancy finished her note and left it on Dawn's desk. Just as she closed the door behind her, she bumped into Stephanie, who was still in her running tights and jogging bra.

"Oh, um—Dawn left her door open," Nancy said, pointing back into the room.

Stephanie crossed her slender arms and pursed her pouty lips. "Uh-huh, that's a new one."

Nancy held up her hands in mock surrender. "You're right, Steph. Actually, I just broke into our R.A.'s room. I was after the secret files she's keeping on all of us. You do know about them, right?"

Stephanie rolled her eyes.

Nancy noticed Stephanie's bare stomach and shoulders. "Nice outfit, Steph, but isn't it getting a little chilly for that? Or does working up a sweat keep you warm enough?"

Stephanie tossed her hair. "I have to go," she said breezily, and slipped by.

"Coming to the pasta party?" Nancy called.

Stephanie leaned on one hip. "Why should I?"

"I heard you were hanging around the registration tables today. You could even keep your workout clothes on. I'm sure no one would complain."

Stephanie flashed Nancy an unamused smile. "I don't have time for a pasta dinner with a bunch of scrawny runners."

"I don't know," Nancy replied, trying hard not

to laugh. "Looking at all the gorgeous guys in line today, I thought you'd fit right in."

Stephanie twirled a lock of black hair around her finger. "Maybe," she said. "I'll think about it."

Nancy winked. "You do that."

Stephanie stared at her slinky image in the mirror. She ran her fingers over her stomach. It wasn't the rock-hard washboard it used to be.

"Maybe I *should* start running," she murmured. "Not that I *really* need to," she quickly added.

As much as she hated to agree with Nancy, some of those guys at the race registration weren't half bad. Though maybe a little too skinny.

Stephanie pulled on a gray sweatshirt, sat heavily on her bed, and lit a cigarette. She was feeling strange vibrations as she scanned her room, stopped at her desk.

That stupid picture, she thought.

She reached over for the 8 × 10 glossy blowup of her father, R.J., with his new, his new— Stephanie couldn't bear to think the word.

"Wife?" she said with a grimace.

She'd gotten it in the mail Thursday, with a note from the new wife herself, Kirsten. It was signed with only about a dozen *X*'s and *O*'s.

The problem was, "Mom" was hardly older than Stephanie. Okay, maybe ten years sounded like a lot, but Kirsten was only twenty-eight, and her father was over fifty!

Not that Kirsten even looked as old as twenty-eight. She could have passed for a Wilder student in a second.

"Young—and not stupid," Stephanie murmured. "Moving in on the old Keats fortune." But Kirsten kept smiling back woodenly, as if she hadn't heard a thing, forever frozen in whatever blissful moment she and Stephanie's father had been in.

Stephanie smoked her cigarette down to a stub, not even bothering to open a window so that her roommate, Casey Fontaine, wouldn't have a fit about the smoke. She lit up a second cigarette and calmly lifted the picture and tore it in two, watching the pieces flutter into the trash.

"That's better," she said, falling back against her satiny sheets. Horrified, she blinked away what she thought might have been a tear.

"A lot of good that REACH meeting did me yesterday," she muttered. "I don't know why I even mentioned my step-hag problem to Dawn. I suppose because she's the R.A. I must have thought she'd be someone to talk to. And all she did was take me to that silly off-campus meeting. The whole thing was a waste of time."

Except, she had to admit that the group leader—or whatever he called himself—was incredibly handsome. That curly brown hair and glowing hazel eyes. Mitch something. Mitch—Lebo.

Everyone at the REACH meeting seemed to be convinced that he had all the answers. "Rules for life," he'd called them. Stephanie wasn't interested in rules. "Excuse me," she'd drawled, "but rules cramp my style."

And it was weird how everyone kept chanting about love and friendship, and that it was important to sacrifice for the friends who loved you. Yeah, right, thought Stephanie, your REACH friends.

"Some great gift of philosophy," Stephanie murmured. "All you have to do is spend about a lifetime reading all the books Mitch has written to understand it. What a gift. That's like going to detention."

Stephanie eyed the photo torn cleanly between her father and his new wife that was in the trash.

"Reach for love, sure," Stephanie said. "I'd sooner reach for stepmommy's throat!"

Dawn Steiger could hardly sit still, she was so excited. She'd put on her favorite dress for the occasion, a knee-length flowery sundress that showed off her long, slim body.

She was surrounded by young people just like herself, a bunch of them crammed together on the big overstuffed couch and on the floor at her feet. Most were students at Wilder, but others said they came from Weston and other nearby towns.

At the group's insistence, Dawn had just finished telling them how she'd been feeling less confident lately, how her studies had been suffering, and how she'd been slacking off on her responsibilities as an R.A. Then she told them that she thought it had to do with her incredibly painful breakup with a guy she really loved.

"If *he* left *you,* it sounds like he could use a little REACH himself," Mitch Lebo said, smiling.

Dawn lifted her head. "Thanks for saying that," she said softly.

"But it's true," Mitch insisted. "You don't believe me. Look how beautiful you are!"

Dawn blushed and felt a little surge of self-confidence return. It was the first positive thing she'd felt about herself in weeks.

She had to admit, Mitch was the most charismatic person she'd ever met. A little older than they were—he wouldn't divulge his age—but Dawn guessed he was around thirty. He was strongly built and had a square jaw and sensitive, hazel eyes with golden flecks that seemed as if they could see right through her. Sitting alone on a chair in front of a big picture window, Mitch looked as if the ribbons of sunlight that streamed in all around him were coming *out* of him, as if he had magical powers.

To Dawn it seemed that whatever she needed to hear, Mitch said it. Whatever she was thinking, Mitch also seemed to think it.

"When someone lashes out," Mitch was telling the attentive group, "he's really lashing out at himself. Anger is frustration, and insensitivity is really selfish love."

He's unbelievable, Dawn thought. And smart.

Mitch was like a magnet. All eyes were on him: everyone, both men and women, looked at him with adoration and total respect.

Someone grabbed Dawn's hand and squeezed it. It was a young woman Dawn had seen around campus last year. Beaming, Dawn squeezed back. She felt more at home here than she'd ever felt, even at her own house with her parents. The group had told her that every afternoon was set aside for love-bombing: focusing loving attention on one person, listening to that person's problems, helping her find solutions.

It was kind of an initiation, they'd said. And while it sounded a little weird, Dawn had to admit it was incredible. For the first time in weeks, she felt accepted and loved.

"Just one more thing before we break," Mitch said. "A new group on campus, Earthworks, is doing some great educational work about the environment. I'd just like to say that it's a very positive group and worth our support. We may have a lot of work ahead of us here, studying the REACH precepts and concentrating hard on our personal growth, but don't let that stop you from getting involved in something so worthwhile. If any of you are runners, or joggers, the Ten-K race on Sunday might be fun."

Grinning, Mitch surveyed the room. "Just a thought. Have a great day, everyone!"

I will, Dawn said to herself as she got to her feet. REACH, and Mitch Lebo, are just what I need.

CHAPTER 3

Early the next morning, as Nancy set up the 10K registration table in the lobby of Thayer Hall, she glanced up to see a group of her suitemates making their way down to the cafeteria.

"Hey, you slackers!" Nancy called out. "None of you guys have signed up for the race yet!"

Casey Fontaine, tall and willowy, with short red hair, cringed. "Not so loud, Nance, we haven't had our coffee yet."

"If it was a Ten-K *crawl*," Ginny Yuen said, "I might consider it."

"Or a Ten-K bakery stroll—" Reva Ross tossed in.

Kara laughed. "Jelly doughnuts every quarter mile!"

"Okay, okay," Nancy said. "I get the point. But I expect you all to donate at least ten dollars to Earthworks. And to come to the pasta dinner tonight to support those with more *courage.*"

Casey groggily saluted. "Aye, aye, sir!"

Nancy noticed that Kara was beaming more than usual. "Having trouble keeping up with all your new runner boyfriends, Kara?"

Reva winked. "Oh, they were all just harmless flirtations," she said, imitating Kara's voice.

"Well, of course they were," Kara said defensively. "I was only being friendly."

"But that's not what poor Tim thought," Eileen O'Connor, her brown hair still wet from her shower, said in a stage whisper. "You missed him, Nance, because you were down here. He showed up at the dorm this morning with such a lost puppy-dog look on his face."

"Yeah," Reva added. "Kara had made the mistake of giving out her number to another Alpha Delt."

Kara's face went tomato red. "It was just to give out information about Earthworks," she protested.

"Anyway," Kara said, regaining her composure, "Tim thought I was going to dump him or something. Crazy, huh?"

"Yep," Nancy agreed, laughing. "Where *do* these boys get all these crazy ideas?"

"Well, he left all smiles," Eileen teased, patting Kara on the back.

"I didn't expect any of those other guys to ask me out," Kara explained.

Just then Nancy noticed Casey's fuzzy slippers. "Nice slippers, Case," she said, and laughed.

Casey's green movie-star eyes flared dramatically. "They're from Charley, and I love them."

Charley Stern had been Casey's costar when she'd starred in a hit TV series. He was dropdead gorgeous, incredibly sweet, and Casey's real-life boyfriend. The mention of Charley's name usually gave everyone a chance to tease Casey about her TV star boyfriend.

"Charley Stern," Reva said dramatically.

Ginny raised the back of her hand to her forehead. "I can't bear it."

Casey had wandered off. "You're all *so* dull," she said, waving behind her. "Meet you guys at the chocolate-chip pancakes."

Nancy let the others go only after they promised to come to the dinner that night.

"Hi, big-shot."

Nancy turned around to find George cradling a stack of race forms. She was smiling from ear to ear. The night before Nancy had finally caught up with her by phone and told her the news.

"So, did you dream up your acceptance speech for your first journalism prize?"

Nancy held her chin in thought. "Yeah, I was thinking Pulitzer."

George nodded, equally serious. "Good choice."

"Being a full reporter is going to be so great," Nancy said happily. "All those interesting people to meet, fascinating places to go—"

"All that *typing*," George added, cringing. She cleared her throat and handed over the forms. "But on to more urgent matters—"

"Good," Nancy said. "I was just running out of registration stuff."

"I brought someone with me to help." George nodded to a young woman beside her with reddish brown hair. Nancy could tell she was a serious runner from her shape.

"This is Kate Terrell," George said. "She runs middle-distance on the track team."

"Hi," Nancy said.

"Hopefully George'll also be part of the team soon," Kate said, smiling.

A look of worried concentration crossed George's face. "If I really kick butt tomorrow."

"I've never seen you be anything less than sensational when you're motivated," Nancy assured her.

Kate nodded. "She'll definitely be one of the strongest runners on the team."

"I have to get *on* the team first," George reminded them.

Kate had started pulling old flyers off the bulletin board to make room for race posters. "Here, let me help," Nancy said, grabbing the colored paper.

"Wow, these guys really get around. They have flyers up all over campus," Kate said. In her hands was a yellow sign, saying, REACH—Support, Understanding, Peace.

Nancy glanced over. "Oh, yeah, I saw them out on the quad yesterday. What are they all about?"

Kate raised an eyebrow. "Spooky."

Nancy stared at her. "What do you mean?"

Kate sighed. "Let me put it this way: I wasn't

off to a great start this semester. My grades were flat, my times on the track were way down, and I was kind of lonely. Life in general pretty much stunk. I heard about REACH. Supposedly, it was about helping students meet new friends, gain perspective on their lives, and generally how to be happier and stuff."

"Sounds great," Nancy said.

"Yeah, great." Kate sneered. "I went to a few of their meetings. The guy who runs them is incredible, Mitch Lebo. He's passionate and committed, not to mention totally gorgeous. He was such a good speaker I couldn't take my eyes off him."

George picked an old REACH flyer up off the floor. "*Totally* gorgeous?" she said. "Where do I sign up?"

"Don't bother. After a while everyone just seemed kind of creepy," Kate continued. "I couldn't put my finger on it. It was like they were under some spell. Then they wanted to love-bomb me—"

"Love-bomb?" Nancy laughed. "Are you serious?"

Kate shrugged. "They wanted me to spill my guts in front of thirty total strangers."

"Sounds thrilling," Nancy quipped.

"So what'd you do?" George asked.

Kate thumbed toward the door. "I was out of there in two seconds flat, but they kept calling me and knocking on my door—trying to get me back. They kept it up for two weeks. Then they got bored, I guess."

"Actually—" George said, squinting into the distance, as if she were trying to picture something. "They sound like the same people I've seen giving speeches in front of the Student Union—"

"And outside the Copacetic Carrot," Nancy added, suddenly remembering seeing them outside the health-food restaurant.

"Come to think of it," George said, "last week Will was talking about some guy he'd heard about—some guru dude who was starting to develop a really big following on campus."

As Nancy cleared some more space on the bulletin board, she found another REACH flyer. It had the same wording as the *Wilder Times* ad in Dawn's desk drawer.

I wonder if that's where she's been, Nancy thought.

Then she remembered how Dawn's room had seemed so eerily empty.

"Boy, those people were weird," Nancy overheard Kate mutter.

Maybe I should talk to Dawn, Nancy thought.

Later, after George and Kate left, more students started lining up to register. Gary Friedman, a *Wilder Times* photographer, showed up at the table, waiting patiently in line, his hands behind his back.

Gary gave her a huge smile. "Hi, Nancy," he said.

"Hi, Gary," Nancy replied, chuckling because Gary was smiling so hard. She looked up at his slightly overweight, out-of-shape body. "You don't want to sign up for the Ten-K on Sunday, do you?"

"Me? Have no fear," Gary replied. He whipped his arm around and stood holding a bouquet of flowers exploding with purples and reds and yellows and lots of white baby's breath.

"They're beautiful!" Nancy gasped.

Gary handed them to Nancy.

"For me?" Nancy choked. "Uh, thanks, Gary, but what's the occasion?"

"There's a card."

Nancy saw that her name on the little envelope was written in Jake's handwriting and tore it open.

Hey Miss Reporter—you're pretty AND smart! Congratulations! Call me . . . Jake.

"These are so sweet," Nancy said, burying her nose into the blooms and inhaling deeply. And *he's* so sweet, she thought.

"But how did he get you to come all the way over here?" she asked Gary.

"I owed him for something," Gary admitted. "Better this than having to bring him cheese-steak subs at three in the morning during one of his on-deadline all-nighters."

"He couldn't deliver it in person?" Nancy probed.

Gary just shrugged. The problem was that she wanted to give Jake a huge hug. She'd been waiting to give him the news face-to-face and to revel in his congratulatory kisses. Gary wouldn't do as a substitute.

I guess Jake's just too busy, she thought.

She was going to tell him the night before, but Jake and his roommate Nick had a long-standing date to go to a pro basketball game in Chicago. The tickets had been hard to get and cost a fortune.

Jake had offered to meet her later, but that would have meant waiting up until about one or two in the morning. Because she had to be up so early to set up the registration table, Nancy passed.

She studied Jake's card.

"It's obvious he knew ahead of time," she thought aloud. "But I still can't figure out how. Especially since I haven't met with Steve Shapiro yet. In fact, according to Gail, the promotion isn't even official."

Nancy squinted. How *did* he know?

A week or so earlier Bill Graham had called Dawn's room. When he didn't get an answer, he'd smiled at her usual cheerful greeting on her machine and left a message asking her to a rock concert at the Field House. If she wouldn't be his girlfriend, they could at least hang out together.

Besides, who knew? Maybe in time she'd see what a wonderful, loving guy he could be.

But she never called him back. He left another message, which she'd finally returned with a message of her own saying she couldn't make the concert because she had to study. Besides, she said, she couldn't afford the ticket. She didn't even say thanks for asking.

The third time he called, he asked why she needed to study on a Friday night, and that if she felt she couldn't afford the ticket, he'd happily pay for it. Though he didn't say it, he also wanted to know why she'd sounded so spaced out.

This time—which must have been the fifteenth time in the past week that he didn't get an answer—he just listened to the long beep after her greeting and sighed. Then he put down the phone.

"What is with her?" he said out loud, lying back on his bed. "It's like she's on another planet. First she bags out on the concert. Then she's spending all her time with this group she talks about. And she blows off our R.A. meeting last Sunday *and* our usual cup of coffee afterward."

Bill ran his fingers through his short red hair. If it was just him she was ignoring, he wouldn't have liked it, but at least he would have understood. But according to Dawn's friends, she was canceling plans right and left to hang out with the REACH people.

Bill let his head rest against the wall. "I know losing Peter was devastating to her," he thought aloud. "But I wish she had *some* time for me—as a friend."

Bill hopped to his feet and started for the door. "Well, getting depressed over Dawn is making me hungry."

Bill was crossing the first-floor lounge when he stopped dead in his tracks. He spied Dawn heading for the doors, lugging a stuffed duffel bag. But *was* it Dawn? For a second, Bill wasn't positive. There was something different about her. As long as he'd known her, she'd always been in great shape. She had a swimmer's muscular limbs and back.

But this Dawn was thinner, and her beautiful, flowing hair was uncombed and dull, as if she'd just gotten out of bed.

"Dawn!" Bill called.

Dawn didn't break her stride. "Oh, hi, Bill," she said breezily.

" 'Oh, *hi*, Bill'?" he repeated. "I've been trying to get you for days. Didn't you get any of my messages?"

"I'm really sorry. I'm just so busy lately. I haven't been able to return calls. I only stopped by for a few minutes to grab some clothes." She was speaking so quickly, Bill could hardly understand what she was saying.

He reached for her arm. "Dawn? Slow down—"

"I can't. I'm on my way to—"

"A REACH meeting, I know," Bill said, exasperated. "But just give me a sec, okay?"

Dawn stopped, but her eyes were on the doors.

"What's going on?" Bill challenged her.

She still wouldn't meet his eye. "Nothing," she said defensively.

"Look, there's a pasta party for the Ten-K race tonight—"

"What race?"

Bill cocked his head. "The Ten-K race, for Earthworks! It's tomorrow. Haven't you seen the signs around campus?"

Dawn shrugged. "I've been kind of busy."

"Right. Well, there's a big pasta party for the runners tonight. It'll be fun. Relaxing, and good food."

Dawn glanced longingly at the doors. "I can't, Bill. I don't have the time. I have an evening study session at REACH tonight."

"Tonight?" Bill repeated, confused. "But it's Saturday. I didn't know there were REACH people in your classes."

Dawn rolled her eyes. "Not for my classes," she said, irritated. "It's for—"

When she finally looked at him, it wasn't Dawn behind the eyes. They were the eyes of a stranger. "Forget it," she said. "You wouldn't understand."

"Look, let's just hang out tonight," Bill said quickly. "Just you and me. I'll skip the party."

Dawn twisted her arm free. "I said no. Besides, I don't have the money for a pasta party—"

"I'll pay your way, Dawn," Bill said.

But it was too late. Dawn had darted through the double doors and was jogging down the walk toward the road, where a green sedan had just pulled up. A door opened and Dawn slipped in as the car pulled away. Through the back window, Bill could make out the heads of four or five other people.

He shook his head. "Something's wrong. No

matter how supportive those people are—" He didn't finish the thought. He just repeated the same thing over and over. "Something's wrong. I know something's wrong."

"Cool T-shirt!" Kara said enthusiastically as Montana walked into the cavernous Pi Phi kitchen in a black baby-T that showed off her slim waist. It had Go Climb a Rock printed in yellow across the front.

"Really, you like it?" Montana asked, charmingly oblivious.

Kara looked horrified. "Do I *like* it? Do I *like* it? Am I *breathing?*"

"She wants to borrow it," George pointed out.

Kara nodded in agreement.

Montana squinted at her. "You ever rock climb?"

"No, but if I can borrow that shirt I promise to learn."

"Hey, guys, you think the linguine's ready?" George cut in. "Come on. It's almost six o'clock."

Pam stuck a long fork into a huge vat of boiling water. She dangled three strands of limp spinach linguine in the air.

"What are you doing?" George asked.

"Hold on, there's a science to this," Pam deadpanned. She flung the fork upward. The pasta hurtled end-over-end toward the ceiling and hit with a smack.

George was nodding, her arms folded. "Uh-huh."

Pam stood under the spaghetti and peered up at it. "If it sticks, it's done."

"I see, Dr. Miller," George said. "Is that a special skill you developed, or were you blessed with it from birth?"

"Blessed," Pam joked. "Definitely blessed."

"Hey, Nikki, great necklace!" Kara said toward the door. "Could I borrow it sometime?"

George looked up. In the doorway stood a small, thin woman with long, gorgeous black hair parted in the middle that played up her delicate cheekbones. She wore a funky skirt of bright red handwoven fabric and a gauzy shirt. Around her neck was a wild necklace made of chunky colorful beads.

So that's Nikki Bennett, George thought. She'd heard a lot about her. Kara had told her she usually walked around campus barefoot. The rumor was that her parents were rock 'n' roll singers in the 1960s.

Nikki smiled. "Of course, Kara." She held out her arms, as if anything on her body that Kara wanted, Kara could have.

"Kara, I couldn't have dreamed up a more perfect place for you," George said, laughing. "You can borrow to your heart's content."

"Yeah, no one locks their closets," Montana threw in. "Everything's fair game."

"Except boyfriends, I hope," Kara said.

Nikki and Montana shrugged and burst out in laughter.

George rolled her eyes. "Well, then, I'm glad *I'm* not pledging Pi Phi."

"You'd better be," Kara said. "With that hunk of yours, I'd be first in line."

"Hey, Fayne!" Pam cried, handing over a heaping bowl of linguine and clinking its rim against hers in a pasta toast. "Carbo-loading commencing. All systems go! We're ready for the crowd."

"All systems go!" George said enthusiastically. "And tomorrow may the best woman win!"

Nancy paid for her jumbo coffee at the counter at the Cave and searched the snacketeria for Professor Shapiro, the *Wilder Times* faculty advisor. A few of the slate tables were occupied by architecture students, slumped over their coffees with circles under their eyes. Most of the tables were empty, though; almost the entire campus was either at dinner or off starting to get ready for an exciting Saturday night.

"Nancy!"

Nancy looked up, but instead of Professor Shapiro, she saw Bill Graham walking toward her.

"I'm glad I ran into you," he said quickly.

Bill's lips were drawn into a tight straight line. He looked worried.

"Is everything okay?" Nancy asked, glancing around distractedly for Professor Shapiro.

"Actually, I sort of followed you here," Bill confessed. "I really need to talk to you."

"I'm kind of in a rush—but what is it?" Nancy asked.

"It's about Dawn," Bill said sadly. "She's acting really strange lately. I ran into her today, and she looks so tired and skinny. And she missed an R.A. meeting last Sunday, which is totally unlike her. There's something weird going on with her. Just between you and me, I don't know if that REACH group is doing her any good. They say they want to make you happy and healthy, but Dawn is looking worse and worse. And she's not taking any time out to have fun."

Nancy gave Bill's shoulder a supportive squeeze. She knew he really liked Dawn, and wanted to go out with her. And he also knew that Dawn didn't necessarily feel the same for him.

The fact was that Bill was in love with Dawn and didn't make a secret of it. And love, Nancy knew, made you see what you wanted to see. Bill was seeing Dawn-without-Bill, which in Bill's eyes wouldn't be good no matter what.

Then again, Nancy thought, Bill is always so calm and levelheaded. Then she remembered what Kate had said about REACH that morning.

"I'll tell you what," she said. "I'll keep an eye out for her at the pasta party tonight, and I'll talk to her and see what's going on, okay?"

An is-that-all? look crossed Bill's face before he nodded reluctantly. "Okay," he said. "But I doubt you'll have any luck. She didn't even know there was a party tonight. And when I told her, she said she couldn't come."

"That's weird," Nancy said. "It's her kind of party."

Bill nodded. "I know, I know. But she said she had something to do at the REACH house tonight."

Nancy's eyes widened. "Really? Like what?"

"She said they were studying. Can you believe it? On Saturday night? And then she said something about money—"

Nancy caught the eye of Professor Shapiro, who was sitting at a small corner table. He gave her a little wave.

"I've got to run now," Nancy said quickly. "I'll talk to her. Promise. Catch you later."

"Yeah, later," Bill said unenthusiastically as Nancy spun away.

Professor Shapiro was wearing a gray tweed jacket and was smiling warmly. As little as Nancy knew him, she liked him a lot. He was pretty young, just a couple years out of grad school, so most of his students in his journalism courses and the writers for the *Times* thought he was incredibly cool. And hilarious. Jake said Shapiro did great impersonations of historical figures and that he usually had his students in stitches by the time his lectures were over.

"Hi, Professor Shapiro."

"Call me Steve," he replied, pushing out the extra chair with his foot. "So—I hear you're quite an impressive writer. The first freshman to make full reporter. This meeting is to make your promotion official."

Nancy became suddenly afraid. Something in his voice made her doubt that he'd promote her.

But Steve was smiling at her, as if he'd zeroed in on her fear. He touched his coffee cup to hers. "Congratulations," he said. "You're officially a reporter."

A surge of enthusiasm rushed through Nancy. She had the urge to wrap her arms around him, even though she knew it wouldn't be appropriate. But it was really Jake she wanted to embrace.

I can't wait till tonight, she thought.

"So tell me about some of your pieces," Steve said.

"Well, you read them. What do *you* think?" Nancy laughed. "You're the expert."

Steve nodded as if considering. "From what Jake says, you're already pretty accomplished."

"From what Jake says?"

Steve nodded. "He's a real fan of yours. I've only had a chance to look at one of your first pieces, the football interview. It showed promise. But Jake's a good friend, and he doesn't stop talking about you."

"Well, then, did you talk to Professor McCall, my journalism professor?"

"I see Dan all the time," Steve said amiably. "But I have to admit, the last time we met, your name didn't come up."

Nancy looked at him. "But you did make the decision, right? I mean, my promotion's definitely okay with you?"

Steve shrugged, smiling. "Of course. It seems that you'll make a crack reporter. And since Jake thinks so, and Gail, I agreed. I trust their judgment implicitly. You should be very happy."

"Of course I am," Nancy said, though without meaning it. Something was bothering her.

First Jake gives me this strange, knowing smile *before* I go in to talk to Gail, she thought. Then he sends me flowers *before* the promotion is official—or even public. Now Steve Shapiro doesn't seem to be too concerned about the actual work I've done. And he can't stop mentioning Jake.

Nancy knew that Jake and Steve were friends, but now it was sounding as though they'd talked over her promotion before it even happened.

Steve held out his hand. "Look, Nancy, I'm only there to advise. It really was Gail's decision. Don't worry."

"'Gail's?' 'Worry?' Why would I—" Nancy repeated.

Steve's laughter interrupted her. "I know, I know. Gail's a hard nut to crack sometimes. Jake and I have butted heads with her in the past."

Nancy cocked her head. "And you had to butt heads with her over this?"

Steve burst out in laughter. "You really are an excellent interrogator, I see. No, I didn't have to butt heads with her exactly. After I talked to Jake, maybe a little friendly persuasion."

Nancy felt something inside her drop, as though something had fallen off a shelf.

After he talked to Jake? she thought. Gail needed to be persuaded? But by whom? Steve Shapiro—or Jake?

Suddenly the gleam on her promotion was gone. It didn't seem as if she'd earned anything. It seemed as if someone did someone else a favor—and it wasn't her!

CHAPTER 4

Even before she reached the Pi Phi house, Nancy could hear the party in full swing. Music filled the cool evening air. Every window was lit up. The wraparound porch buzzed with conversation and laughter.

In the party room, tables were filled with bowls of spaghetti and sauce and steaming trays of garlic bread. Kara, Montana, and a few other Pi Phi members were rushing around clearing empty bowls and bringing in new ones.

Nancy almost missed Jake in the chaos. He was dressed in baggy jeans and an old flannel shirt, but since this was a running crowd, he fit right in.

George was standing next to him in running shorts and a blue V-neck sweater. They were with a couple of freshmen reporters and some other people she'd never seen before.

When Nancy walked up, they were all deep in

conversation. Jake gave her hand a squeeze. Nancy told herself to squeeze back, but she couldn't.

Just being near him, Nancy felt her heart begin to pound. Jake was like no one she'd ever known—handsome, but just rough enough around the edges to keep her slightly off balance.

Then why didn't I return his squeeze? she wondered. That had never happened before.

Because you're angry, Nancy reminded herself.

She couldn't get her "interview" with Steve Shapiro out of her head. Jake definitely had some explaining to do.

Tuning into their conversation, Nancy guessed they'd be talking journalism, but then she heard Jake say, "I have to admit, REACH sounds like it's doing great things."

"Yes," George agreed. "And it's terrific that REACH is getting so involved in the environment. It makes sense that one group should support another."

"Well, the world is really one big community, and we're all part of it," one of two guys Nancy assumed were in REACH said.

Everyone stood there nodding, including Nancy.

REACH doesn't seem so weird, she decided. Maybe Bill's just lovesick after all. She noticed that the REACH members were nice looking, athletic, dressed in sweats and sneakers. Totally normal.

Nancy caught George's eye. George lifted her

brows and shrugged, as though she was wondering what Kate had meant, too.

"A bunch of us are running tomorrow," one of the REACH guys said. "In fact, we all got together to donate a hunk of money to Earthworks."

"Wow!" George said. "I don't know what to say."

"Say you'll come hang out with us one of these days," one of the REACH members said.

"You're all invited," a woman from the group said. "Anytime. Come by after the race if you want. Our house is just off campus. You can't miss it. It's an old Victorian we fixed up."

Suddenly Nancy thought she saw Dawn across the room. She craned her neck—it was Dawn's hair all right, long and straight blond. But when the girl turned around, it was someone else.

Nancy looked at the REACH guys. "Do you guys know Dawn Steiger?"

"Sure." A young man waved his hand. "She's around here somewhere, I think. She said she was coming, anyway."

"Oh, good," Nancy said, a little relieved. Bill must have gotten confused. The REACH group seemed really nice. Maybe Bill *was* just jealous.

"If you see her before I do, let her know I'm looking for her. I'm Nancy."

"Nancy?"

Nancy smiled. "Nancy Drew."

The man shook her hand warmly. "I'll be sure to tell her, Nancy. But right now I'm starving. Come on, guys. Let's get some of that pasta!"

Watching the REACH members walk away, Nancy said to George, "They're okay."

"I know," George agreed. "REACH seems interesting."

Out of the corner of her eye, Nancy could see Jake smiling at her. She cleared her throat. "Can I ask you a question?"

"Sure," Jake replied.

But before Nancy could say a thing, she was buttonholed by her Thayer suitemates.

"Nancy," Reva said. She had a bowl of pasta in one hand and Andy Rodriguez's fingers in the other.

"Great hair!" Nancy said. Reva had braided her hair into long ropes.

Andy grinned enthusiastically. "I approve."

"Though Eileen's a little worried that it might keep her up at night when I turn over," Reva said. She twisted her head, making the ropes slap together.

"Hair like that would drive me up a wall," Stephanie muttered.

"Nice to see you here, Steph," Nancy said. Stephanie was wearing a white bodysuit that accented her richly tanned skin and left almost nothing of her slinky body to the imagination.

"Plans fall through?" Nancy teased.

Stephanie waved blithely. "I just thought I'd drop by."

"Come on, Steph," Reva chided her. "Confess! You're actually having a good time."

"Not really," Stephanie replied.

Turning to the others, Reva lowered her voice

in a stage whisper: "I actually saw her laugh—once."

"Yes, at all these Earthworm do-gooders," Stephanie sniped, "talking about saving the world."

"It's Earthworks," Andy corrected her. "And don't think I didn't catch you joining in the fun a few minutes ago."

"In your dreams," Stephanie grunted. "And what *are* those REACH creeps doing here? What rock did they crawl out from under?"

Nancy looked at her. "You know about REACH, too?" she asked.

"Yeah—the losers."

Nancy smiled. Surprise, surprise. Stephanie thought they were losers. The fact was, Stephanie thought *everybody* was a loser. Being a loser in Stephanie's eyes was almost a compliment. At least she noticed you.

Looking at her, Nancy suspected that below her suitemate's tough-as-nails attitude was someone else dying to escape, someone who could even be—was it possible?—nice. From their only serious conversation, even though it was a brief one, about Stephanie's father and new stepmother, Nancy was also pretty sure that the tough exterior was hiding as many fears and worries about family and future as everyone else Nancy knew.

"They are so cute together," Reva said, interrupting Nancy's reverie.

Nancy turned and saw George and Will against the wall. They had carved out a little private space for themselves and were lovingly sharing a bowl of spaghetti, their eyes flashing.

A snicker escaped Stephanie as she covered her eyes. "I can't bear it. Can you believe she's actually feeding him?"

"Have you ever seen two people so in love?" Reva asked.

Yes, Nancy thought automatically. She turned toward Jake. "Can I ask you that question?" she started to say.

Jake, deep in conversation with someone else, impulsively turned and took Nancy in his arms. He lifted her chin, and for only a second she resisted. She really needed to talk to him. When Jake bent to kiss her, the party noise floated away, far away.

"But I have something to say," Nancy tried to get out, but she was stopped by his lips. She wasn't complaining. Her questions would have to wait.

Bill couldn't even remember the name of the girl he was talking with. She was nice. She was even pretty. And he definitely noticed the Lycra running singlet she was wearing, and the floral scent of her perfume. . . .

But the fact was, he couldn't keep his eyes away from the door. He kept hoping Dawn would show up, and that she would suddenly be standing and looking for him. He'd even slapped on extra aftershave and put on the blue shirt with wavy lines that Dawn once had laughed at, just so she'd notice him.

When he saw George and Will walking arm in

arm, he felt a tiny pang of jealousy. Once, in a weak moment, Dawn had let him walk her to the dorm with an arm around her shoulders, and he'd never forgotten the soft but firm touch of her, or the silky warmth of her skin.

"Bill!"

He whirled around. "Dawn!"

But it was Nancy.

"Have you seen her?" she asked.

Bill shook his head. "I told you she's doing that REACH thing tonight."

"But some REACH guy said she was here," Nancy said.

Bill shrugged. "Really? Where? I don't see her anywhere."

Nancy shrugged. "Somewhere—I guess."

Bill was just about to ask her about REACH when someone backed into him, one of the freshmen in Dawn's suite—the woman in the white bodysuit.

Nancy cleared her throat. "Do you guys know each other?"

But Stephanie had sidled around to Bill's side, and her hand was already in his. "Stephanie Keats. Isn't this party *droll?*" She lit a cigarette, blowing a thin stream of smoke past Bill's handsome face.

Bill choked. "Should you be smoking those things in here?"

"You're so right," Stephanie drawled, linking her arm in his. "I could definitely use some fresh air."

Bill felt Stephanie's sultry brown eyes on his

face and smiled stiffly. "S-some air would be nice," he stammered. "I guess."

"Stephanie!" Reva called, slipping through the crowd. "There you are. You know Andy and I have been wanting to know why you dropped your computer lessons."

Bill knew that Reva and Andy had set up a computer consulting business in Andy's apartment.

"I heard something about your getting really good," Nancy said.

"I'm just taking a break," Stephanie replied. Bill noticed her giving him an embarrassed glance.

"But we *so* look forward to your company," Andy added sarcastically.

Bill caught Reva throw him a wink. That was his signal for his getaway.

Thanks, guys, Bill thought to himself, happy for the interference. There was no doubt that Stephanie was totally hot and might even be a lot of fun, but the only company he wanted right then was Dawn's. And Dawn wasn't showing. He was sure.

He started sidestepping toward the door.

"But what about that drink?" Stephanie asked.

"I thought you wanted some air," Bill said over his shoulder.

"I meant air," Stephanie corrected herself. "I do."

Bill glanced longingly at the night outside. "Send me an e-mail, and we'll set something up."

* * *

Nikki nodded approvingly at the silver frog on Kara's shirt. "That pin looks awesome."

"Thanks to you," Kara replied cheerfully. She turned to Montana. "You should see all the cool stuff she has."

"You don't have to tell me," Montana said. "Her closet's like a little store. And you know what Nikki says—share and share alike."

Kara's eyes widened. "Everything?"

Montana nodded. *"Everything."*

Suddenly Kara felt a hand on her hip. She turned slightly and saw the longish brown hair and cute mouth of her boyfriend, Tim Downing. Kara's suitemate, Liz Bader, had introduced them because she said they had the same upbeat personalities—and she was right. They fit each other perfectly.

Tim was staring at Kara's shirt. "Nice frog."

"There's more where that came from," Montana cut in.

Kara was about to laugh when she saw the suggestive look on Montana's face. She noticed Nikki's eyes traveling up and down Tim's body. Innocent little Nikki? Then she remembered Nikki's parents, and thought of all the wild partying of the sixties.

Did Tim's eyes really flash?

It's just your imagination, Kara told herself. Montana and Nikki are your sorority sisters. They'd never flirt with your boyfriend.

But then Kara blinked. Tim, Nikki, and Montana were laughing hysterically. Nikki leaned against Tim's shoulder. Montana slapped his back. And they'd only met a minute ago!

"Yeah, share and share alike," Kara heard Montana whisper.

"Wow, I ate so much spaghetti," George complained, pressing in her stomach, "I don't know if I can run tomorrow."

"I know," Pam added. "That wasn't just carbo-*load*ing, it was carbo-*over*loading."

"Excuses, excuses," Will said.

Jamal snorted in agreement.

The four were strolling down the hill from Pi Phi, back toward the center of campus. Kara, Nikki, and Montana had relieved George of any cleanup duties so she could get a good night's sleep and be ready for the race.

"By the way, now that your race will be over tomorrow," Will said to George, tightening his squeeze on her hand, "maybe you'll help me with something."

"Anything," George said.

"Wilder is starting a series of student-curated art shows," Will said. "And I've been thinking about putting together a proposal for a show."

Pam whistled. "Sounds great."

George rested her head on Will's shoulder. "Count me in," she said lovingly. "But maybe the day *after* tomorrow? I have a feeling I'm going to need to rest my legs."

"You sure will," Pam joked.

George squinted at her through the dark. "Is that so?"

"Yes," Pam replied, laughing.

"You want to know what I think?" Will asked quietly. "I think you're each other's best competition, but if you don't stop talking and start doing, your mouths are going to drag you down and neither of you is going to win."

No one said a word as they passed the outdoor basketball courts where pickup games went on all day. The sound of one ball bouncing—*ping-pa-ping*—echoed in the dark. In the far corner, some guy was practicing foul shots.

"Maybe you two should just settle this score like a couple of men," Jamal suggested, stopping to stare at the courts.

George and Pam glared at him. "And what's *that* supposed to mean?" Pam asked.

Jamal smiled slyly. "It means a fast game of one-on-one."

"Us?" George asked.

"Why not?" Jamal answered.

"Maybe that's not such a great idea," Will suggested. "I mean, you guys are going to be racing in less than twelve hours—"

"And you're afraid we'll hurt ourselves?" George asked, giving him a playful slap. "What do you think we're made of, glass?"

"Yes, the era of the fragile female on a pedestal is long gone, boys," Pam said. "Nothing like a little one-on-one between friends, right, George?"

George nodded eagerly.

"I don't know about this—" Will said tentatively.

"Oh, come on," Jamal scolded Will.

"But only on one condition," Pam said. "If George and I are going to settle this like *men*, then you have to be *women* and cheerlead."

Jamal waved weakly. "Rah," he said limply.

George nodded. "Okay, you guys pass."

Jamal jogged over to the guy dribbling on the far court and talked him into lending them his ball for a few minutes.

"Okay," he said, passing the ball to Pam. "Game to eleven."

Will crossed his arms. "Are you two sure you want to do this?"

George ran over and kissed him on the lips. "I love you, but be quiet and cheer."

George couldn't remember the last time she played basketball, but she wasn't bad. Neither was Pam. Laughing and goading each other, they played pretty evenly, with George staying a point ahead.

Jamal and Will had gotten into it, clapping and whistling for their respective girlfriends.

George had the ball. Suddenly she really wanted to win. She needed one basket, and she was going to get it. But she could tell Pam really wanted to win, too.

Why am I surprised? George wondered. *I'm an athlete, and so's Pam.*

Will and Jamal were watching intently.

George eyed the basket, then sprinted around Pam. As she went up for the layup, Pam knocked into her. The ball rolled around the rim and fell out. On her way down, George called foul.

As her feet hit the ground, a searing pain ripped into her ankle and up her leg. The pain was so intense, George collapsed on the court. "My ankle!" she cried. "I think I broke my ankle!"

CHAPTER 5

I can't believe it's already eight in the morning, Dawn thought to herself. I haven't eaten or slept in two days, but I'm not even tired. In fact, I'm totally energized.

The sun was pouring through the windows of the off-campus REACH house. A dozen or so students were sprawled on the floor, chins in their hands, intently reading through stacks of books, In an adjoining room, a half-dozen more were sitting around a dining room table, studying the REACH principles of happiness. It could have been a library or a reading room, except that every book had been written by the same author—Mitch Lebo. And every book was published by the same company: REACH, Inc.

"Evil is loving yourself before loving your family," Dawn overheard someone recite. She'd been hearing that all night, and after the fiftieth time, she had begun to understand and agree.

Someone else said, "REACH *is* family."

Dawn looked up from her spot on the floor. The people around the table were the advanced REACH members: Mitch's trusted aides and teachers-in-training.

"Maybe I can be one of them someday," Dawn murmured hopefully. But her own hopes surprised her. She'd been coming to meetings for almost two weeks now, but until yesterday, she had doubts. Now she was totally convinced that REACH was for real. And so was her commitment to it.

"Are you hungry at all?" she asked a girl named Jill. Jill was new to the group, too. She was tall and pretty, and had also just broken up with a guy.

"I can't even think about food," Jill replied.

Dawn turned her head to the window. The sunshine seemed to match her sunny outlook.

I can't believe I ever doubted how good these people are, she thought. Or how much they care about me. It's almost as if it took a whole night of studying and reading and talking for me to see how good REACH is.

"REACH *is* my family," she murmured. Her eyes stung with hot tears. She and Jill faced each other, and, as if Jill had just reached the same conclusion, they hugged tightly. She felt as if she were home.

Dawn noticed the people at the table in the next room staring at them and beaming their approval. She glanced around her, and for the first time in weeks felt totally free of the pain of losing Peter.

A car pulled up outside the house, and Dawn hopped to her feet. Mitch was moving up the walk, followed by three of his oldest followers.

Dawn felt a smile creep across her face. Mitch was wearing a pair of faded jeans and an old, frayed jacket. Dawn used to like clothes. She once liked to dress nicely, and every now and then she'd go down to Selina's and splurge on something expensive, but Mitch didn't seem to care much about clothes.

As he entered the house, Dawn could feel herself wanting him to notice her. Mitch was incredibly attractive, and she gravitated toward him as toward a magnet. But it was more than his looks. It was the way he saw with his eyes, and the way he walked. As if he knew something.

But what? Dawn wondered. What does he know that I don't?

"Hi, Dawn," Mitch said affectionately. "I see you noticed what I'm wearing."

For a second, Dawn was spooked. She *was* thinking about his clothes and how ratty they were.

How does he know what I'm thinking?

Mitch lifted his voice to lecture level. "Don't forget that appearance is nothing. It's just a shield."

Some of the others had come in from the adjoining rooms. Dawn felt the good vibrations of everyone around her. Jill took her hand.

"Don't forget how monks live," Mitch said. "When they enter the monastery, they give up everything, except their souls. You need just enough money to eat, to live. Any more is a luxury, and when you're studying and fulfilling your inner dreams, you can't afford material luxuries."

Mitch turned toward the rest of the group. "Who's running in the race today?"

Six or seven people raised their hands.

Mitch smiled. "Good luck. But don't forget that it's not whether you win or lose . . ."

A few of them starting laughing. "We know, we know, Mitch. It's how you run the race."

Everyone laughed, and Dawn felt a jolt of happiness.

Mitch bowed his head. "Let us pray for their success and safe return," he said. They all bowed their heads at once and squeezed their eyes shut.

After a few minutes someone else spoke up, "We met a few interesting people at the Earthworks party last night and invited them over."

Mitch nodded. "Excellent. The more the merrier."

One of the older members stepped forward. "Dawn and Jill were studying very hard last night, Mitch," he said.

Mitch turned his hypnotically beautiful eyes on Dawn, and she quickly looked away. He reached out and squeezed her hand. "I'm proud that you had such a productive night, Dawn," he said soothingly. "In fact I came here this morning to thank you for signing the personal contract with me and demonstrating your commitment to the group."

Dawn smiled. Last night, when they brought the contract to her, she wasn't sure what it was, and whether she should even sign it. It was before her desire for food had completely vanished, and she was kind of spaced out from hunger. She'd also taken something they'd given her—a small pill. They'd told her it was an herbal wake-up pill, totally natural and healthy, to help her concentrate.

Then they told her that Mitch himself had asked her to sign the contract—to "seal her covenant." She tried to read it carefully but got tired halfway through and skimmed the rest. By the time she signed, there were four or five people surrounding her, watching her.

I can't believe I ever doubted the contract, Dawn thought to herself.

"That was the most important document you'll ever sign," Mitch said.

Dawn nodded. *Yes,* she thought.

"And you've been incredibly generous, Dawn. But I feel the need to reach out farther into the Wilder community. As beautiful as you are, there are more lonely people trapped where you came from. You must know some, don't you?"

Suddenly Dawn felt everyone looking at her. *Do I? Who's Mitch talking about?*

"I guess so," she said tentatively.

"Well," Mitch agreed. "We need pamphlets and flyers and advertising space to get those lonely people to hear us. That takes money unfortunately."

Dawn felt everyone's eyes on her. No one was saying a word.

"Well," she began shyly, her heart pounding, "I'm getting another paycheck first thing tomorrow morning for my R.A. salary. I could give that. I mean, it's not much, but will it help?"

Dawn felt a dozen hands rubbing her back. Mitch stepped forward. His strong hands reached out and held her face gently, and he leaned down and kissed her softly on each cheek, lingering just long enough for her to take him in totally, feel his hair rubbing against her, smell the sweetness of his breath.

I love you, she wanted to say, without knowing why. He just seemed to fill every crack in her heart.

She held her own breath until he pulled away, smiling, his eyes gleaming with wisdom.

"Today's a new day for you, Dawn Steiger," Mitch told her. "And a whole new life full of love—and happiness."

"There you are," Nancy said as she and Bess stepped through the doorway to Will and Andy's apartment. They each carried a box of doughnuts.

Nancy swallowed. "We went over to your room, but you weren't there."

"That's because I'm here," George said sullenly.

"I guess so," Nancy said, uncomfortable at seeing her always cheerful friend not so cheerful.

"So how's the patient? Does she want a doughnut?"

George picked a chocolate one out of the box and took a bite. She was sitting on Will's couch in her sweats with her leg propped up in front of her. A big bag of ice sagged on either side of her wrapped foot. She was staring blankly at the TV, which was flickering silently with a Sunday morning program.

"No race, huh?" Nancy said.

Her arms crossed, George shook her head.

Bess reached for George's foot and caressed it a little. "Does it hurt?"

"Only when you touch it," George growled.

Will grabbed two doughnuts for himself. "But it's not broken. The doctor at the clinic said that she was lucky she got away with only a bad sprain."

"You forgot to say that a sprain can be harder to heal than a break," George mumbled.

Will spoke softly to Nancy. "She hasn't exactly been looking on the bright side of things this morning. I think it's finally sunk in that she isn't running today."

"I heard that!" George said.

"Well, you're still lucky," Bess insisted. "You could have broken your foot." She reached for George's aluminum crutches and hobbled around the room with her left foot in the air.

"Wrong foot, Bess," George pointed out. She raised an eyebrow at Nancy. "And maybe it didn't have anything to do with luck."

Nancy's mouth fell open. "What's that supposed to mean?"

"I thought *you* came down on *Pam's* foot," Bess said, lifting her right foot in the air.

"She did," Will said. Then, turning to George he added, "I told you it wasn't a good idea to play so hard."

"And I told you not to say 'I told you so'!" George shot back.

Nancy knew her friend so well, and she knew that even though George sounded angry, she was really disappointed.

There was a knock on the door. Nancy opened it. Pam and Jamal were standing there. Pam was wearing a yellow running singlet that showed off her well-defined shoulders and powerful thighs. Her running number was pinned to her front. Jamal was holding a bouquet of flowers.

George stared at them stonily.

"No go, huh?" Pam said, obviously disappointed.

George shook her head silently.

"I'm really sorry, George," Pam said.

But the look on George's face stopped her. "Uh-huh," George said.

"What does that mean?" Pam said, confused.

"Why wouldn't you want me to run?" George said accusingly.

"George!" Will cried.

Pam obviously wanted to say a thousand different things, but she only narrowed her eyes. "I'm your roommate, and your friend. I can't *believe* you think I'd—"

Pam couldn't finish her sentence. She stalked out of the apartment.

"Pam, stop!" Jamal called out after her. But Pam wasn't stopping. He turned to George. "It's nobody's fault," he said tightly. "She'd never do that on purpose, and you know it."

"That doesn't change the fact that there's no way I can race," George said through gritted teeth. "Now I probably won't make the track team. Without a good qualifying time in a sanctioned race, my chances as a freshman are almost nil."

"That doesn't change the fact that it was an accident," Jamal said tensely before walking out.

Nancy couldn't believe what she'd just seen. "But how could Pam have done it on purpose?"

George shrugged.

"Why don't you get on your crutches and hobble over with us to the race," Nancy suggested.

"These things aren't so bad," Bess said, crisscrossing the room on the crutches. "At least they're not wooden and heavy and uncomfortable. These are sleek and kind of cool."

"Yeah, real cool," George grumbled. "Forget it. I'm not going."

"I bet Pam could use the support," Will said reasonably.

"I bet she could," George replied sourly.

Bess, twirling her blond hair around her finger, clucked her tongue. "You can't be mad forever."

"But I can be mad for a little while."

"Well, even if you won't watch the race, there's

still the Earthworks party," Nancy said, trying to cheer George up.

George grabbed a big throw pillow and hugged it protectively to her stomach. "They'll just have to get along without me," she muttered.

The room filled with unhappy silence.

Nancy cleared her throat. "Doughnut anyone?"

Bess and Nancy passed the basketball courts on the way to the 10K starting line. Tight knots of sweaty, shirtless guys were streaking up and down the pavement. Suddenly one face popped out of the basketball crowd: Paul's. All he had on were a pair of sweats, a tank top, and basketball high-tops. Bess's eyes were glued to him.

I know I'm busy, Bess thought to herself. I know I promised to focus on my work, but he is *so* good-looking. And he has been so nice to me.

"Earth to Bess?" Nancy was saying.

Bess blinked. "Huh?"

Nancy smiled. "See something you like?"

"Just browsing." Bess laughed.

"Hey, you see what I see?" Nancy suddenly asked.

Bess followed Nancy's gaze toward the far court. There was Jake running up and down with the ball. He was one of the best players, but he moved awkwardly.

"He's so cute," Bess said dreamily.

"And so very strange." Nancy laughed.

"But in a good way," Bess insisted. "I mean, who else on campus plays basketball like that?"

Nancy shook her head. "Absolutely no one," she admitted. "He's unique. And I *have* to talk to him."

"What about?" Bess inquired.

Nancy shook her head. "There's something I have to clear up. We didn't have a chance to talk last night."

"No doubt," Bess cracked. "How could any words have slipped out of those smooching lips."

Speaking of smooching, her eyes secretly cut back to Paul. He'd just stolen the ball from someone, streaked the length of the court and dropped in an easy shot. He was lithe and graceful.

Yes, you're a cutie, too, she mused.

"Excuse me, excuse me, coming through," Will said as he pushed through the crowd to help George hobble over to the sidelines of the race.

George rolled her eyes. "Thanks, but please stop making such a fuss over me."

"Okay. But I'm glad you decided to come cheer Pam on."

George grumbled. "I'd rather torture myself by watching a race I should have won than sit at home eating the rest of that box of doughnuts."

Will smiled crookedly. "I hate to break it to you, George, but you already ate the whole box."

George looked mortified. "The *whole* box?"

Will nodded.

"Great, if I can't make the track team, I may as well try out for the Goodyear blimp."

Will kissed the top of her head. "Stop whining. Watch the race."

The streets were lined with students. The lead pack of runners was just rounding the bend, about to hit the halfway mark.

"Here they come!" someone screamed.

George used her crutches for support and craned her neck. She expertly sized up the race. There was her friend Kate, running easily at the head, just where George expected her to be. Her stride was even, the swing of her arms powerful but efficient.

"Kate's a total pro," George said. Will nodded in agreement.

"Where's Pam?" he asked.

He's right! George thought. Where *is* Pam?

The lead pack was streaking by. Pam should have been with them, shoulder to shoulder.

Then the middle pack came by and finally George caught sight of Pam's yellow singlet. Whenever George ran with her, she couldn't help but notice what a natural athlete Pam was. She was built for speed. Not long-distance, like George. But in an all-out sprint at the finish line, George knew she'd never be able to take her.

But Pam was nowhere near the finish line now. She was a solid minute and a half behind the leaders!

"She's having a terrible race," George muttered. "What's wrong with her?"

Pam glanced into the crowd as she passed. George stiffened as they made brief eye contact. Pam didn't smile or nod—she just glared. George looked away, embarrassed that she'd said what she did back at Will's apartment. But she couldn't undo it. Besides, she *was* still annoyed that she wasn't running, and that her future with the track team was in jeopardy.

Pam snapped her head forward, eyes down. There was no sign of that killer instinct—that desire to win. It was as if she were out for a morning jog.

George swallowed hard.

"I know she's a better runner than that," she said, unable to hide the disappointment in her voice.

"So does she," Will added.

CHAPTER 6

That's what I like about these Sunday morning R.A. meetings, Bill thought to himself as he gathered up his things—they start on time and end on time.

The R.A. advisor, Agnes Murphy, was really nice but a stickler for rules.

As Bill headed for the door, Mrs. Murphy waved him over. She'd always been friendly and helpful, but always insisted that her R.A.s act responsibly. Bill walked toward her slowly; he knew what was on her mind.

"Bill?" Mrs. Murphy asked. "Where was Dawn this morning? This is the third meeting she's missed."

Bill shrugged. "Maybe she's at the Earthworks Ten-K race."

"Are you telling or guessing, Bill?"

Bill cringed inwardly. He didn't like to lie, but

he felt pulled by his loyalty for Dawn. "I don't know, really," he replied. "But I'm sure it's something serious. Dawn is very responsible, especially about being an R.A. I'll do my best to find out what the problem is."

"If you're her friend, you will," Mrs. Murphy agreed. "Because if she really cares about being an R.A., she'd better come to see me. If she misses our next meeting, she's out of a job."

Bill shook his head as he watched Mrs. Murphy leave the room. She may have been a slave driver, but this time around, she had a real reason to be upset.

Dawn was completely slacking off on her responsibilities. She'd missed three meetings already, and Bill knew she had no idea what was happening in her own suite. Not that there was anything brewing there. The women in 301 were great, and none of them was really in any trouble. But that wasn't the point. Dawn was supposed to be there for them and she wasn't.

Bill was trying to understand, to give Dawn the benefit of the doubt. He knew new friends were important to her, but her commitment to them was now interfering with her commitment to the suite, not to mention jeopardizing her job!

Well, there's still *my* job to worry about, Bill sighed. And I may as well pick up my paycheck, since I've also got bills to pay.

Bill took the flight of stairs up to the second floor to see the accountant, who came in on Sundays to see that they were paid. Bill's calendar and schedule had been checked at the meeting;

he'd kept track of all his required hours as an R.A. Everyone's schedule was then signed by Mrs. Murphy.

Even though Dawn hadn't turned in her schedule the week before, Bill knew Dawn would get a check this week, just as she'd get one next week—if Mrs. Murphy didn't fire her.

Usually, Dawn and he went to the office together to pick up their checks. Maybe she'd already come by, he thought.

At the desk Bill showed his student ID and signed for his check. The crisp white envelope came sliding back across the counter.

"Do you think you could tell me if Dawn Steiger has been by to pick up her check?"

"Hasn't been in yet," the woman said as she checked the log. "You two usually come together."

"Right," Bill mumbled, hoping he didn't look as bothered as he suddenly felt.

"Actually," the woman said, as she flipped back through the log, "there's a note here about Dawn's money. I don't have a check for her at all."

"She hasn't been fired?" Bill began.

"Oh, no," the woman explained. "She came in last week and made new arrangements for her money. I'm not getting a check for her because she's having it go direct deposit into the University Credit Union."

"Direct deposit to her bank?" Bill asked. "Why?"

The woman shrugged. "Who knows? She

doesn't have to say. But she won't be coming here for it anymore, if you were hoping to see her."

"No," Bill said quickly. "I was just checking."

What's going on, Dawn? Bill wondered. "You've been so spaced out lately you can't meet any of your responsibilities, yet now . . ." Bill stopped at the bottom landing, and nodded, as if something suddenly made sense. Now you're not too spaced out to take care of your paycheck?

Instead of inspiring her, the sound of heavy breathing all around her was making Pam feel claustrophobic and sluggish. Her legs kept pumping, and she heard the sound of her feet hitting the ground, but she felt jerky, disconnected. It was almost as if she were watching herself in the race rather than running in it. And why would she want to be a part of it, way back in the middle of the pack with the second-string racers?

Pam tried to concentrate, to get back her stride, but every time she tried to focus, all she could think about was the one-on-one game the night before with George. Pam tried to remember. Did I really hit George's arm? Wasn't she playing just as hard as I was playing?

Pam asked herself one last question as she struggled to stay in the race. I was already down, the game was almost over. Why didn't I just let George win?

But it wasn't my fault, Pam wanted to scream, as one more runner passed her on the outside. No way did I do anything on purpose. Pam felt a surge of anger as she remembered George's face, twisted with the accusation that Pam had hurt her to get rid of the competition. The anger seemed to speed her up for a moment.

But then right behind the anger came the hurt—hurt that her roommate and friend would accuse her of something so mean.

Pam surveyed the bobbing heads and shoulders in front of her. She was at least a minute behind the leaders, maybe even two. Nothing could help her win now.

But maybe this will convince George I didn't hurt her on purpose, Pam couldn't help but think. When she finds out how badly I did. Just then Pam glanced at the sidelines and almost stumbled. There was George! Staring right at her.

George's eyes were wide, and her mouth started to open. Pam couldn't quite hear with all the noise around her. Then George's mouth closed, and she didn't say a thing.

Not a thing.

At the last second Pam was hoping she'd hear her friend shout out some encouragement—to show her that she still supported her and wanted her to do well. But obviously George didn't want her to do well. She probably wants me to drop out, Pam thought.

Well, no way am I going to give her the satisfaction. Some friend, Pam almost choked, as she felt the anger surge through her as she made her way through the small pack she was in toward open space, and the leaders.

Me quit? This race isn't over.

Pam finally felt her legs fall into their smooth pumping rhythm, felt the wind whistle by her ears. I'm not just watching, saying nothing. I'm *in* this race!

Thanks for everything, George. And nothing.

Thayer Hall was quiet. It was midday Sunday, and everyone was either outside in the sunshine, or in the library getting ready for classes.

Not Nancy. Nancy stood facing her full-length mirror, picking at the long-sleeved shimmery dark green tunic again. She frowned, twisting one way, then the other. The shirt was made of that great new bouncy rayon-spandex fabric, and while it looked simple, the shirt was deceptively sexy: it clung to every curve and moved easily as she moved. Would it be *too* sexy? Did she really want to draw that kind of attention to herself?

"Yes," Nancy whispered, thinking of Jake. That night Jake was going to clear up the whole confusion about her promotion. It would turn out to have been a harmless miscommunication.

At least I hope so, a small voice nagged at her.

"All right!" Kara's voice cut into Nancy's reverie as her head popped into the doorway. "Come on, guys! We've got a little fashion show going on in here."

Embarrassed, Nancy glanced over to where her roommate stood in the doorway. Kara winked as Nancy smiled and blushed.

"I guess you're getting ready for tonight's bash, too, right?" Kara chatted as she came into the room followed by her two Pi Phi sisters, Montana and Nikki.

"Yeah," Nancy said, and sighed. "Only I—"

Montana held up her hand. "Wait. Let me guess. You don't have a thing to wear."

"Well, Nancy," Kara said, pointing at Montana, Nikki, and herself, "let the fashion police guide you."

"Yep, give it up," Nikki agreed, motioning Nancy to come closer. "What are the options?"

"Well, this that I have on," Nancy started.

"Can you put a little something behind that, Nan?" Kara teased. "I feel like I'm looking at something on a hanger. Let's see how it moves."

Nancy laughed and struck a pose or two, twisting so that the shirt bounced and clung.

"And it does move," Montana agreed. "If you aren't going to wear it, *I* will."

"We're here for Kara's closet, don't forget," Nikki reminded her. "Option two?" she asked Nancy calmly.

Nancy picked up loose denim overalls and a terra-cotta scoop-necked T-shirt.

"It's more casual, I know," Nancy began.

"It *is* earthy," Montana said, obviously trying not to smile.

"If you want to look like you were just outside weeding," Nikki added.

"It's cute," Kara translated. "But a little too country for a party. Lean toward sexy," she suggested. "It really suits you better."

"You think?" Nancy mused, looking back in the mirror at the green tunic.

It *was* attractive. And sexy, but she wasn't sure.

"So let's see what you've got hidden in here," Nikki murmured, turning her attention toward Kara's closet.

Nancy chuckled as Kara's Pi Phi sisters ransacked Kara's closet.

"Wait!" Kara cried, trying to stop Montana's long arm from snaking toward the back of the closet. "There's nothing good back there, really." But Montana was already oohing over a little red linen dress she'd unearthed.

"I use the there's-nothing-good-back-there line, too," Nikki said, winking at Kara.

"You're not saying I can't borrow this, are you?" Montana asked, almost aghast.

"Of course not," Kara replied quickly. "Only I didn't think you'd like it. It's kind of casual. Very simple."

"Well, I love it," Montana decided, clutching the dress tightly in her hands.

"It's hard to take, isn't it," Nancy commiserated as she pulled on her slim black jeans to wear with the green tunic top.

"What?" Kara almost couldn't bear to tear her eyes away from her clothes.

Nancy nodded toward Montana. "A taste of your own medicine," she teased.

"Oh no," Nikki replied quickly. "She doesn't mind. Share and share alike, right, Kara?"

"Right," Kara said miserably.

"Oh, Nancy! You look totally excellent!"

Nancy whirled around. Bess was in the doorway, flushed and out of breath, her bright blond hair windswept and mussed. "Can I borrow your brush before we go?" she asked almost without pause.

"Sure." Nancy laughed. "You can even come in and catch your breath."

Bess almost fell into the room and collapsed on Nancy's bed after saying hi to the three Pi Phis. "I feel like I haven't slowed down all day," she moaned.

"You look like it, too," Nancy teased. "What's up?"

"Sorry I'm late." Bess smiled, as she crossed her feet. "Ahhh. That feels *so* good."

"Hey," Nancy joked, perching herself on her desk. "Take a load off. Tell me all about it. What's up?"

"Oh, Nancy," Bess said. "Well, first it's the Kappas, there's some big sorority thing I can't talk about except to say we had a bunch of rules and lectures."

"Learning all the trade secrets?" Nancy smiled.

"Exactly," Bess admitted. "Then I had a matinee of *Grease!* And then I had to do some studying. . . ."

"You, studying?" Nancy cried. "Minutes before a party?"

It was still hard to get used to this "new Bess" routine. Nancy couldn't imagine Bess sitting still with her books for more than a few minutes at a time.

"Well, having my awful, horrible, terrible, nasty roommate is good for something," Bess admitted.

"Like a studious environment?" Nancy asked.

"Yes," Bess replied. "Upon penalty of death."

"Now there's a woman who needs to go to a good party," Nancy said. Leslie King was premed and practically insane with academic ambition. She and Bess were about as opposite as two people could be, and though they were joking about her, Nancy knew that for Bess, it was pretty hard living with Leslie.

"I actually did invite her tonight," Bess admitted. "Though I don't know why. She just about had a heart attack at the idea of not studying every second of every day."

Bess hopped to her feet, went over to the dresser, and ran a brush through her hair. "Ready when you are," she said, tugging through a knot.

Nancy jumped up from the desk and grinned as she hooked her fingers in the collar of her leather jacket.

Nancy nodded at Kara, Montana, and Nikki on her way out. "Later," she tossed over her shoulder.

" 'Bye," Bess added.

Montana and Nikki waved over their heads, poring through the contents of Kara's jewelry box.

"I just want to check one thing," Nancy said as she and Bess walked into the lounge.

She stepped over to Dawn's door and knocked. There was no answer. Nancy decided to try the door. Maybe Dawn hadn't remembered to lock it again?

The knob turned easily. Nancy stepped into the room. It looked exactly the same as it had on Friday.

Nancy scanned the room, spotting the note she'd left for Dawn about the pasta party. It was still on the desk, exactly as Nancy had left it. There was even a faint line of dust along the table when Nancy touched the paper.

"This is weird," Nancy murmured to herself. "Where *is* she? It's like she's totally vanished or something."

Nancy shook her head. No point in leaving another note about the party, Nancy realized. From the look of things, it could be spring before Dawn saw it.

Dawn's absence around the suite the last week or so was too strange. Something was going on with this REACH group, Nancy thought, remembering Kate's warnings about them. Even if the REACH members at the party had seemed nice. Something's definitely up—and I'd like to find out what it is.

"Oh, this is incredible!" Montana cried, twirling in front of the long mirror, the linen sheath hugging her figure.

"This, too," Nikki agreed, admiring the wide black pants, bodysuit, and funky leather vest she'd borrowed. With her long glossy black hair, she looked as if she'd stepped right out of a western.

"Now all we need are shoes and jewelry," Montana agreed.

Sighing, Kara tried to smile. She really liked her new friends in Pi Phi. And she loved how generous they were—though she hadn't expected it to backfire like this.

Kara stared longingly at the other side of the room.

"Oh, Nancy," she mumbled. "I never really appreciated you until now. Someone to borrow *from,* not *with.*"

"What was that?" Nikki asked innocently. "You want to borrow something of mine? Anything in my closet," Nikki added. "You know that. Anything at all."

That was the problem, Kara realized, suddenly depressed. Not that she didn't want to lend Montana and Nikki her stuff. It's just at this rate, everything she owned would be in their closets. And the anything-at-all creed would apply to the little red dress and her favorite vest, too.

Nikki was so spacey, Kara knew she could lend Kara's stuff out to other people. Then Kara would never see the stuff again.

Unless she was lucky enough to spot it on some unsuspecting student. Already Kara could imagine passing a stranger in the library and noticing that she had on Kara's earrings, pants, or shoes. All Kara would be left with were a pair of old loafers and a sundress from high school.

Keep your eyes open, Kara silently commanded herself, until all your stuff is safely back here, where it belongs.

CHAPTER 7

The tightly packed crowd at Pi Phi roared and clapped when Kate Terrell walked in through the front door of the sorority with a victor's wreath on her head. Pam also clapped—twice.

"You *could* be a little happier for her," Jamal said, hanging back with Pam against a far wall. "After all, she is your friend."

For the hundredth time that day, Pam felt near tears. "Of course I'm happy for her. Kate's a great runner. She deserves to win. But—"

"You're not thinking about Kate."

Pam kissed Jamal on the lips. "Thanks for reading my mind," she said. "It makes it a lot easier when I don't feel like talking."

Jamal had been incredibly sweet about the whole thing. He'd listened without taking sides and spent the night and held her to comfort her while George was at Will's apartment recuperating.

After the coach of the track team placed a medal around Kate's neck and the winner of the men's competition, the lights went down and the Pi Phi living room became a shadowy mass of dancing bodies. The floor buzzed with a thumping beat, and the melodies were funky and fast. Hip hop, rap, and funk—just the kind of music Pam liked to get down to, especially with Jamal. In fact, she'd fished out her sexiest dress for the occasion, something that would let her dance the night—and her pent-up energy—away.

Jamal was looking really hot tonight in white jeans and black T-shirt.

But as much as she tried, Pam's mood was anything but festive.

"I still can't believe she thinks I did it on purpose," she muttered.

Jamal gave her hand a squeeze.

Pam tried to smile. "Thanks for understanding. I know I'm kind of dead tonight."

Jamal leaned over and nibbled on her ear. "But a sexy dead person, all the same. But, hey, did you see George at the finish line after the race?"

"Yeah, I saw her," Pam replied dryly.

"I think she wanted to congratulate you."

"Rub it in, is more like it," Pam scoffed. "And don't butter me up," she warned him. "That was the worst race I've ever run, and you know it."

Jamal was moving his hips, obviously dying to get out on the dance floor.

He shrugged. "So what? You still placed in the top ten. They'll be begging you to try out for the track team. By then you won't be so mad and you'll do some serious whomping."

"So will George, I hope," Pam replied, suddenly not knowing whether she hoped George would do well, or was afraid she would.

Jamal smiled and tickled Pam under an arm. "So you're not so mad all of a sudden, huh?"

Pam slapped his hand away. "I'm mad. I still can't believe George thinks I'd hurt her on purpose. She wouldn't even cheer for me today. Not a peep. But that doesn't mean I hope she never runs again."

"I have a theory," Jamal announced, and cleared his throat. "George was looking forward to running the race so much, she was so psyched, that when she got hurt, all her energy came out directed at you as anger. But it wasn't really anger. It was frustration. Remember at the clinic how she looked like she wanted to cry. Well, what do you think?"

"Of your theory, or George?"

"Either," Jamal said. "Or both."

"Good theory, bad George. I'll never forget what she said. Never."

Bess raised her arms, lifted her face to the ceiling, and laughed. She was dripping sweat, feeling the hip-hop beat travel up her legs and through her body. Hips swaying, hair flying, she was dancing harder than she ever had. And the funny thing was, she was dancing in a circle of girls, next to Nancy.

"This girls-only idea is excellent," Casey Fontaine, one of Nancy's suitemates, screamed.

Bess gave her the thumbs up. It was fun to take a break from guys and dance with girls.

A slow dance came on, and the dance floor cleared a little. Bess and Nancy and Casey and the others walked over and leaned against a wall, laughing and breathing hard. Casey left and came back with a half dozen cups of something jammed in the crooks of her elbows.

"Where'd you learn to do that?" Bess asked. "Don't tell me you ever waitressed."

Casey nodded. "In a real greasy spoon, just before I did my screen test for *The President's Daughter*."

"So, the great Fontaine is mortal, like the rest of us," Bess jested.

"Will wonders never cease," Nancy said. Suddenly she waved. "Hey, over here!"

Bess turned, expecting Jake. But this guy was taller, and leaner, and all too familiar.

"Everyone, this is Paul Cody," Nancy said.

Paul smiled and shook everyone's hand. Until he got to Bess. "Oh," he said.

Bess lowered her eyes. "Hi—"

"Boy, it's great to see you again," Nancy was saying. "You guys, Paul gave me a tour of the campus our first week here. He showed me all the ins and outs, and what not to order at the cafeteria."

"Really," Casey said suggestively. "Tell us."

Nancy smiled. "He was the perfect gentleman, I assure you."

"Could this be true?" Casey asked, incredulous.

Paul held up a hand. "Scout's honor. Don't you have a boyfriend, Nancy?"

Bess and Nancy looked at each other, and laughed. "Did," Bess said. "I mean, does. I mean—"

"What Bess means," Nancy said, helping her out, "is that I'm seeing someone else now."

Bess found herself warding off a pang of envy.

Stay focused, she chastised herself. Her pledge to stay away from men was fading in and out. Library, books, library, books . . .

Paul gazed longingly at the dance floor, where couples were moving slowly to the slow music.

"So—" Bess said, fishing for something to say.

But Nancy was looking at her strangely. "Am I off base here, or do you already know each other?"

Paul smiled. "Actually, yes. I mean, sort of."

"Sort of?"

"Yeah," Bess said insistently. "Only sort of."

"Well, it's great to see you again," Paul quickly said to Nancy, obviously not knowing what to make of Bess. "I've been wondering how you were making out at Wilder—"

As Nancy replied, Bess concentrated on her smile. Because if she didn't, she knew it would fall.

Suddenly, Bess noticed Paul looking at her, as if waiting for her to say something.

"So," he said, shifting from one foot to the other. "Lots of free time these days?"

"Um, not really."

Paul looked at Nancy, but Nancy only shrugged. "That's what she says."

"Sorry to hear that," Paul said. "It's a huge loss for the rest of us. You're really sweet and funny and full of life—not to mention beautiful."

"Wow!" Casey said. "Cool me off!"

"Get me air!" Nancy cried.

Bess cocked her head and gazed into Paul's eyes.

Library, books, library, books, she heard in the back of her brain.

Bess could feel the beads of sweat blooming on her forehead.

Whatever you do, don't let him see you sweat, Bess warned herself, quickly drying her skin.

Paul smiled. "I'm serious," he said quietly. "I would like to get to know you better. If you ever do find the time . . ."

Standing shoulder to shoulder, Nancy and Bess watched Paul disappear into the crowd.

"I don't know whether to respect you or think you've lost your mind," Nancy said.

"Option two," Bess replied, shaking her head.

"But why? There's room for a boyfriend *and* school. You just have to make the time for each one."

Bess's eyes were saying, Easy for you, difficult for me.

"Without forgetting the other," Nancy added.

Suddenly Nancy felt herself being tugged away and led onto the dance floor. Another slow song was just starting. She closed her eyes as a strong hand pressed against her back and brought her closer.

She pulled her face back only enough to say, "Wow. Some entrance."

"Don't talk yet," Jake whispered in her ear. "I know you have a lot to tell me, but let me just hold you for a while first."

Nancy was dying to talk, but the thousand thoughts that had flooded her brain spilled out, and she thought of nothing but Jake's lousy dancing and how he kept stepping on her toes.

I have to get him to take some lessons, she thought to herself.

A few minutes later they were outside in the cool night air, strolling on the lawn. Pi Phi sat on a small hill, so the lights of Wilder, and the town of Weston, spread out before them.

Nancy took Jake's hand and brought it to her lips. "I have something to tell you."

"I guess you'll be writing more of your own stuff from now on," Jake said with a grin, "now that you're a full-time reporter."

"You knew from the beginning," she said.

"So?" Jake said, laughing. "Aren't you happy?"

Nancy shrugged, unable to collect all her thoughts. She only had suspicions. "Isn't it a little strange that you knew before I did?"

"Of course I'd know," Jake said. "Gail told you it was an editorial board decision, didn't she?"

"And I met with Steve Shapiro the other day."

Jake smiled suggestively. "Yeah, he really liked you."

"You talked to him?"

"He's great, isn't he?" Jake wanted to know.

Nancy nodded despite herself. Jake wasn't really paying attention to what she was saying, and she was starting to get frustrated.

"Steve mentioned you," she said.

"Yeah, we talk a lot, we hang out sometimes."

"And have you talked about me?" Nancy asked.

Jake kicked at the ground. "I guess. But a reporter never reveals his sources, right?"

Nancy gritted her teeth. "Right. But Steve had mentioned something about Gail's being really stubborn. Did you talk to her about my promotion, too, Jake?"

Jake shrugged. "You know how Gail is. She doesn't like to admit she's a softy. She likes to come off as tough and hard as nails."

Nancy swallowed hard. It was suddenly clear: he had to talk Gail into giving her the promotion.

"It was Gail's decision, right?" she probed.

Jake rocked his head back and forth. "Well, the editorial board always talks about everything. But, sure, every decision is Gail's in the end."

"So you *did* have something to do with it," Nancy said, unable to keep the accusation from creeping into her voice.

Jake reacted with surprise. "I thought you were a great reporter from the beginning," he started to explain. "Why shouldn't I stand up for you?"

"But Steve didn't even mention anything about my writing. Gail didn't say anything, either. She just said a decision was made." Nancy's indignation rose in her throat. "I don't mind your standing up for me—as long as it doesn't mean something else."

"What's *that* supposed to mean?" Jake crossed his arms, all the softness and affection gone from his eyes. "What do you mean, something else? Are you saying I don't take the paper seriously, that I'd support you because I *like* you?"

Yes, that's exactly what I think, Nancy said to herself. But she couldn't say it out loud.

"Maybe you wheedled something," she said tentatively.

"Wheedled!" Jake looked as if he wanted to scream. "You're a good reporter. I mean, a *great* reporter. But I also care about you, *very* much. I can't stop you from being one thing, and I can't stop myself from feeling another thing."

"It can be both, as long as they're separate," Nancy said firmly. "But I'm not sure you understand."

Jake held out his hands. "I don't. I don't see the problem."

"I'm saying I can do it on my own," Nancy said forcefully. "I don't need you to pave the way for me. And if you really cared for me, you wouldn't."

Jake opened his mouth, but nothing came out. Finally he just looked at her sadly, shook his head, and walked off down the hill.

Nancy took a step after him, then stopped herself. She couldn't deny it: for the first time she was incredibly mad—at Jake!

"Hi," Nikki said, grinning from ear to ear.

Kara had known Nikki only a couple of weeks, but she already knew that grin: like a Cheshire cat's, it meant desire, desire for something that Kara had, something that Kara would probably want to keep but could easily be made to lend out of guilt.

Love me, love my sorority sisters, Kara thought.

The dance had kicked into high gear, and Kara had been having a blast. She couldn't believe so many people would come out on a Sunday night! It took long minutes of twisting and ducking to make it across the room to the drinks table, or the bathrooms.

Which is why Tim is taking so long to get back, Kara lamented.

"Can I borrow Tim again for another dance when he gets back?" Nikki asked.

Inwardly, Kara was starting to simmer: she knew that innocent look of Nikki's was a ploy.

Maintain outer calm, she chanted to herself.

After all, these are my new sisters. So what if they borrow my boyfriend for dances as easily as they borrow my clothes?

And what's Tim anyway, except some clothes with a guy stuffed inside?

Nice try, she said to herself. He's only the most important thing in the world to you. Maybe I should hang a sign around his neck: Property of Kara Verbeck.

But she could just as easily imagine the little addendum Nikki and Montana would include: On Permanent Loan to Pi Phi Sorority.

"Oh, here he comes," Nikki said excitedly, peering into the dark.

Kara craned her neck. How did Nikki see him? Maybe she's like a bat and has infrared vision for guys.

The second Tim appeared, Nikki was peering up at him adoringly. "Kara gave you to me for this dance."

"Oh, did she?" Tim replied, throwing Kara an SOS with his eyes.

Kara caught a glimpse of Nikki's bracelet in the dim light. It was silver and had wild-looking spiky things and circles hanging off it.

"Great bracelet," she said.

Tim was trying to get her attention. "Kara—"

Nikki jiggled the bracelet. It sounded like a mini–wind chime. "It's Moroccan," she said proudly.

"Do you think—" Kara started to say.

Nikki was already taking it off.

"Security deposit for Tim?" she said sweetly, putting it in Kara's hand.

Kara winked at Nikki. "Hmm," she said, as though seriously considering the idea.

"Wait a second!" Tim protested.

"If I don't have him back in ten minutes, it's yours," Nikki said.

"Don't I get a say in any of this?" Tim asked.

"You mean you don't want to dance with me?" Nikki said alluringly.

Kara tugged Tim down so she could whisper in his ear: "I love you, but it won't kill you to dance with my friend."

"Just don't expect me to lend you out like a piece of meat," Tim said.

"Deal," Kara said.

Shrugging, Tim went off with Nikki, throwing Kara one last pseudo-forlorn look over his shoulder.

Kara blew Tim a kiss and watched him and Nikki start to dance. Nikki was a great dancer. Soon, they were laughing and smiling.

Kara slipped the bracelet over her hand. It was awesome against her skin.

I never thought of lending out a boyfriend in exchange for goods, she mused, tongue-in-cheek. I'm sorry it didn't come to me sooner.

Maybe things won't be so bad after all.

Nancy was walking extra slowly back to her dorm, taking the long way around the quad. She half-hoped that Jake was hanging around nearby, waiting to make up. She once made a pact with her old boyfriend never to go to sleep until they'd worked out an argument, even if they had to stay up until sunrise.

But I'm right, aren't I? she asked herself as Thayer came into sight. This is too important to me to give in to. Reporting isn't just a hobby of mine. It's as important to me as it is to him.

Sighing, she unlocked the front door, throwing

a last glance back at a bank of weeping willow trees: it would have been the perfect place to wait. But no one was around, and Nancy was exhausted—and hungry.

I hope Kara has something to eat lying around, she thought as she headed down her hall. Someone was standing outside her suite, slumped against the wall. "Jake!" she murmured, her heart leaping.

"Hi, Nancy."

But it wasn't Jake. It was Bill. Nancy tried not to seem disappointed.

"I was hoping to run into Dawn," he said.

"She never showed up?"

Bill shook his head sadly. Nancy looked at her watch. "It's almost one o'clock. You still think she's coming back?"

Bill shrugged. "Still with REACH, I guess."

"But you saw her last night, right?"

Bill looked at her. "How? She never showed up."

"That's weird," Nancy said, squinting down the hall. "Then why did that guy tell me that she was at the party?"

"What guy?" Bill asked.

"Just some guy from REACH who was running in the race. Oh, well, I'll leave a note for her to give you a call."

"You mean she actually answers your notes?" Nancy laughed sadly. "Not lately."

Bill sighed. "I'm absolutely positive something weird's going on, Nance. She missed her third R.A. meeting this morning, *and* I found out she arranged to have her salary direct-deposited into her credit union account. It's like she's going out of her way to make sure she never sees anyone."

"Maybe she just wanted to be able to get to the money faster. People do direct deposit all the time."

Bill was acting frustrated. "But Dawn always said her R.A. salary was enough for her. Now all of a sudden she needs her money faster? And blowing off all her friends, that's not weird?"

Nancy reached out and put a hand over Bill's. She gave it a squeeze. "Don't worry," she said. "Whatever's going on, we'll find out. Dawn has too many friends like you watching out for her."

Bill sighed. "I guess. Only, I wish . . ." Bill shook his head and fell silent.

"You wish?" Nancy asked, raising an eyebrow.

"Oh, you know," Bill muttered. "I'm sure it's written all over my face how hopelessly in love with her I am." To emphasize his point, Bill ran his hands over his face as if to wipe away his feelings.

"With Dawn, you mean," Nancy said softly.

"Yeah." Bill shrugged. "But sometimes it's like she doesn't even see me. I think she avoids looking at me so I won't see the pity in her eyes."

"I'm sure it's not like that," Nancy replied, though she wasn't really sure at all. She just hated to see the hurt on Bill's face.

This was really getting her down. It made her think too much about her last conversation with Jake.

"I just keep hoping she'll open her eyes one

day and see me standing there. Like in a movie or something." Bill let a smile lift the corners of his mouth. "And she'll realize that it was me all along who cared about her the most."

Nancy smiled gently.

"Not that it would hurt to have sizzling good looks," he added.

Nancy took in Bill's short red hair, freckled face, and pug nose. Bill *was* very cute.

Nancy nodded. Though Bill definitely was in love with Dawn, he did make sense about the money.

Okay. It does sound fishy, she admitted. And even if this REACH thing is really cool, why isn't Dawn sleeping in her own room?

"Maybe you're right about Dawn," Nancy said thoughtfully. "I guess if she's spacing out on everything else in her life, why would she suddenly be so concerned about money?"

Bill nodded. "Exactly."

Nancy pursed her lips, thinking. If she does need money quickly, then she might be at the bank first thing in the morning.

"I'll tell you what," she said. "Maybe I'll run some errands in town tomorrow before my morning classes." She winked coyly. "Who knows? Maybe I'll run into her."

CHAPTER 8

The next morning was cool, the sky cloudless. Her backpack slung over her shoulder, Nancy made her way toward College Avenue, the small strip of clothing boutiques, restaurants, and music stores that bordered the campus. Behind her, the campus clock tower chimed nine times, and Nancy started to hustle: the credit union opened at nine sharp.

Inside the bank, Nancy checked out the ATM machines, then looked up and down the long row of windows.

"Dawn," she murmured as she saw a tall, blond woman at the last window. But she swallowed her words. Bill was right—she looked terrible. Her jeans, which used to hug her hips and legs attractively, now sagged and flapped. Her blouse floated unflatteringly around her shoulders. But it wasn't just the way Dawn looked, but the fact that she wasn't alone at the bank.

There was an older, extremely handsome man with her, and two other young people. The man had black hair, and though he was perfectly coiffed and had fine, chiseled features, the clothes he wore were scruffy—an old ratty blazer and baggy corduroys. Nancy recognized one of the young people as the guy who had spoken to her on the quad on Friday.

They must have been waiting at the door when the bank opened, Nancy thought. A little anxious? A little too anxious, maybe?

Nancy started to walk over, then stopped. Dawn was pulling away from the window—with a pile of cash in her hands. She handed the entire pile to the older guy, who smiled serenely and planted a gentle kiss on her cheek. Then he peeled a bill off the top and put it in her outstretched hands.

"This is for you, with our love and gratitude," Nancy heard him say, "for saving countless others."

"Nancy!" Dawn cried, spotting Nancy as the group headed for the door. "I didn't know you had an account here."

"I'm opening one," Nancy said quickly. She stared at the guy.

"Nancy Drew, Mitch Lebo," Dawn said, introducing them.

Mitch smiled.

"Nice to meet you."

"And you," Mitch said, giving Nancy's hands a gentle squeeze. "Dawn told us about you."

Nancy looked at Dawn. "You have?"

Dawn smiled back, brightly. Too brightly.

"Dawn, can I talk to you for a second?"

"We're all friends here," Mitch interjected.

"Of course," Nancy replied cheerfully. "It's just, you know, girl talk."

Mitch's smile wilted, but he nodded reluctantly.

"So where have you been?" Nancy asked quietly as she and Dawn strolled to the other end of the bank. "You look kind of tired. You okay?"

"I don't have the words to tell you how happy I've been lately," Dawn said.

"Really?" Nancy replied, astonished. To her, Dawn appeared exhausted and out of it.

"REACH is the best thing that has ever happened to me," Dawn insisted. "We do all sorts of positive things. In fact, tell George that Mitch was really pushing Earthworks. He goes on and on about how important it is to protect the environment."

Nancy nodded. "That's great."

"But my brothers and sisters are all I have time for now," Dawn went on.

Nancy cocked her head. "Brothers and sisters?"

"REACH is family," Dawn answered. "In fact, I'm thinking of dropping out of school to spend more time studying and helping others learn the REACH ways."

Nancy swallowed. "Drop out?" She noticed Mitch and the others toss over an inquiring glance, and she lowered her voice. "Dawn, are you sure?"

Dawn's eyes flashed. "I've never been more

sure of anything in my life. In fact, you'd love what's going on at the REACH house. Everyone's really smart, Nance. They're your kind of people. And Mitch is—well, what can I say? Words can't describe him or explain him."

Dawn turned and gazed at Mitch adoringly. Mitch gave a little wave back.

Nancy eyed Dawn. "I'll think about it."

"Oh, will you?" Dawn pleaded. She clasped Nancy's hands, then ran back to the others.

"Nice to meet you, Nancy," one of the REACH students said.

"Drop by any time to visit," Mitch added.

After they left, Nancy sat in one of the chairs along the wall and sighed.

I can't believe Dawn is going to quit school for them, she thought. If they really had her best interests at heart, they wouldn't let her. She's obviously giving them money already. Which, come to think of it, is probably why she told Bill she's been so short of cash.

The thought of Bill gave Nancy a hollow feeling in her stomach. And I thought he was just being jealous!

Nancy noticed the clock on the wall. She had only a few minutes to get to her first class.

She hopped to her feet and bolted out the door. But running back to campus, she felt distracted. REACH had given her friend a full-scale makeover—from a beautiful, funny, smart, and responsible young woman to a skinny girl about to lose her job *and* her education. REACH's flyers said they provided love and support. But how could what was being done to Dawn possibly be called support? It sounded more like domination.

Then she remembered the REACH guys she'd met at the party. They were nice, but hadn't they lied? They'd said Dawn was coming to the party when they'd probably known she wasn't. And now this Mitch guy was taking Dawn's money.

"No, something's not right here," Nancy murmured as she bounded up the steps to her first class. "I can feel it."

"All right, all right, keep your pants on," Stephanie grunted as she flung open the suite door. With a pack of cigarettes in one hand, she was wearing nothing but a big T-shirt, which floated teasingly midthigh. "Oh, it's *you*. Are you here for me?"

Bill blushed. "Sorry, no. Is Dawn here?"

Stephanie rolled her eyes. "Dawn who?"

Bill peered over Stephanie's shoulder. "She's still not around?"

Stephanie snorted. "AWOL is more like it. I guess she couldn't hack the Thayer Zoo."

He's so cute, Stephanie thought—and smart. But who needs brains with a bod like that?

"What about Nancy—is she back from class yet?"

Stephanie sighed and jabbed a cigarette in her mouth. "What about Casey? What about Ginny? Would you like to know if the Princess of Wales is in?"

"Well . . ."

"So you never gave me your e-mail address," she said, toying with him.

Bill smiled crookedly. "My what? Oh, that. I'll get it to you, don't worry."

Stephanie smiled a thin-lipped smile that curled at one corner. "Maybe I won't need it."

Bill squinted distractedly. "Can I ask you something?"

"It depends on what it is," Stephanie said.

"Has Dawn ever said anything to you about REACH?"

Stephanie took a deep drag of her cigarette. "You lose. That was your very last chance for a date."

Bill looked confused.

Stephanie reached up and squeezed Bill's cheek. "So cute."

Bill waved the smoke from his face.

"So *that's* where Dawn has been," Stephanie said. "Still with those freaks. Well, it certainly explains some things."

"What do you mean?" Bill asked.

"It's *so* embarrassing," Stephanie said. "I actually let Dawn talk me into going to one of their stupid little meetings. What a waste of time. Love this, love that, respect yourself. But *I* didn't need emotional uplifting. After all, no one dumped *me.*"

At the front of the lecture hall, Nancy's journalism professor, Dan McCall, was droning on and on and on—something about newspapers in eighteenth-century England.

She usually loved to hear about that stuff, but this morning, she couldn't concentrate. Her eyes were fixed on the back of the head in front of her, and her notebook contained only two doodled words—*Dawn* and *Jake*.

Nancy threw down her pencil, and it clattered to the floor. "He's such a jerk," she muttered.

For the first time in a long time, she was in a really grumpy mood. She pondered what might be on the menu for lunch, but thoughts of food only turned her stomach. Maybe this is what it feels like to be Stephanie, she thought.

That does it, Nancy told herself. The second I start thinking I'm becoming like Stephanie, I'm out of here. She stuffed her unopened notebook in her book bag and tossed her pens in after it. But she didn't want Professor McCall to see her leave.

Turn around or something, she commanded him.

Usually Professor McCall filled the blackboard with notes, but for some reason this morning he wasn't writing a thing. Every time it seemed as if he was going to turn around, Nancy half rose in her chair—only to plop back down again as soon as McCall looked up.

After five minutes and six or seven attempts to escape, Nancy finally got her chance and slipped out the door. For the first time, she was cutting her favorite class.

A few minutes later, shoving her way through Thayer Hall's front doors, Nancy's heart was still galloping with frustration and worry.

Upstairs, in her suite, she strode through the lounge, turned the corner toward her room, and ran smack into Bill.

"Stephanie has something to tell you," Bill said excitedly before Nancy could say a thing.

Stephanie stepped out of her room.

"Bill, I'm *so* sorry—" Nancy started to say.

Bill cocked his head. "You are?"

"Yeah, I am. I saw Dawn at the credit union this morning. I think you're right about REACH. Something's wrong, very wrong."

"What did Dawn say?"

Nancy just shook her head. "First, she looks as if she hasn't eaten in days. And that Mitch guy was with her. Dawn gave him her money. A lot. Maybe her entire paycheck."

"She did *what?*" Bill exclaimed.

"That dummy," Stephanie muttered. "Doesn't she know she'll never see that money again?"

"She may never see us again, either," Nancy said.

Bill looked confused. "Why?"

"She said she's going to drop out of school to study with REACH full-time," Nancy said.

Stephanie started to say something, then stopped, an actual worried expression on her face. For the first time in Nancy's memory, Stephanie was speechless.

"She's in deep," Stephanie finally said. "I've seen what goes on in there. That place is bad news. They don't let you eat. They just keep giving you a disgusting molasses drink that makes you sleepy."

Nancy glanced at Bill. "Makes you sleepy?"

Stephanie nodded and told them how Dawn had convinced her to go to a meeting the week before, and how she'd thought they were just a bunch of freaky losers.

"We've got to make Dawn see," Bill said, his eyes wide with panic.

"Yes, you'd better," Stephanie agreed. "I read this article once about groups like that, and it said that the longer you're in, the harder it is to get out. It's like getting sucked down a drain."

"We'll need something definite to show her," Nancy said. "If she *is* under the influence of this group, she'll have to be really convinced that there's something wrong with them before she'll leave."

Listening to Stephanie gave Nancy an idea. "What we have to do is find out what they're really doing in that house, like are they forcing Dawn to give them her money?"

Bill and Stephanie both nodded.

"I'm glad you agree," Nancy said, smiling at Stephanie, "because ..."

Suddenly Stephanie's hands shot up in surrender. "Forget it. No way. No chance."

"But you've been in there before," Nancy pleaded, "and have already been introduced around. You could easily say you've had second thoughts and wanted back in. They wouldn't think anything of it. Please, Steph? We need you."

There was a long silence. Nancy could tell that Stephanie was actually mulling it over.

"She's right," Bill told her. "You have the best chance. Don't you care about Dawn?"

Stephanie shrugged. "She's okay, and I guess it *would* be nice to make that jerk Mitch squirm if I can. He may be the hottest thing in the state, but he's also a slimy snake."

"But it might take time," Nancy warned her. "You'll have to be patient not to arouse any suspicion."

A menacing leer came to Stephanie's face. "What's a little time? Anyone too interested in other people's money deserves to get nailed."

Nancy grinned. Finally Stephanie will be able to use her sex appeal for a good cause, she thought.

"In the meantime, I have to do some research," Nancy said, opening her door and staring at the new computer on her desk. "We'll have to convince Dawn that there's something wrong with REACH by showing her proof from both inside *and* outside. Let's get to work."

Mitch was sitting cross-legged on a table. The REACH members sat on the floor around him, holding hands, eyes closed.

It was so silent, Dawn could hear her own pulse thumping softly in her ears. She gritted her teeth against another pang of hunger. For some reason, after she'd seen Nancy at the credit union, her hunger started to get to her.

"Let me hear it from you now," Mitch commanded, and the entire group chanted the REACH mantra in unison.

"R: Releasing—release your grip on material things and admit your unhappiness.

E: Energizing—energize your spirit by giving to the group.

A: Answering—answer to your fears and weaknesses.

C: Caring—care about others in the group unconditionally and know they care about you.

H: Healing—heal by finishing your inner strength."

Dawn opened her eyes. They were all stretching and squinting into the bright sunlight as if they'd woken from a deep sleep. Dawn felt energized, relaxed. She looked up. Mitch was beaming down at her, and she felt special and loved.

A gray jug was passed to her, and Dawn lifted it to her lips and drank the mixture of water, salt, molasses, and lemon, which was all she was allowed during this long fast that Mitch had put everyone on. At first she'd hated it, but by now, after surviving on it for days, she drank it thirstily. Miraculously, it seemed to quench her hunger, even if it made her feel a little dopey.

"Remember, sustain, but do not indulge," Mitch told the group in his singsong voice. "You're all beyond hunger now. Your bodies are being purified through fasting while your spirits are being healed through love."

Mitch slid down from the table and circled the group. Dawn watched him, feeling herself falling hopelessly in love with him.

Mitch stopped behind Dawn and laid his strong

hands gently on her shoulders. "Don't forget how critical it is to follow the first precept of REACH—you must release your tie to material goods."

Mitch knelt behind Dawn and wrapped his arms around her. Dawn closed her eyes, feeling the warmth of his muscular chest against her, smelling his sweet breath.

"And let us use Dawn as our model," he said. "This morning, she showed how committed she is to our journey. Her donation will let us reach out to others."

Dawn opened her eyes at the knocking at the front door.

The door opened, and Dawn could feel the smile creep across her face as Stephanie walked in carrying an overnight bag.

"Stephanie, you're back!" Mitch said.

"I sure am," Stephanie replied.

Dawn was almost giddy with pleasure. "For good?"

Stephanie nodded.

"You see, everyone?" Mitch announced. "Dawn's friend has returned. That is the power of her love. Dawn is our lucky charm. The day she walked into this house was one of REACH's finest moments!"

CHAPTER 9

Staring intently at her computer monitor, Nancy ignored the campus clock tower chiming noon. Wriggling her fingers over the keyboard, she logged on to her Internet account.

After her father had given her the computer, Nancy had learned how to surf the Internet by using the Internet Guide that Reva and Andy had put together for the university. She'd explored many of the sites on-line and was becoming pretty familiar with certain areas.

"I bet I can get some information about cults here," she muttered to herself as she logged on to one of the information databases.

Yes! she thought as her typing brought up a file heading on religious sects and communities. A list of subjects under the heading showed a file on cults. The file was an index of cult names and leaders, with dates, places, and listings of articles about them.

If REACH has been involved in any illegal stuff, there might be something about it in these files, Nancy thought.

She typed in the commands to bring up the cult file, and groaned—the list was huge! Nancy couldn't believe it. There were hundreds of cults.

"Scary," she said under her breath.

Nancy typed in REACH.

She waited as the computer hummed and knocked, searching the files. The screen flashed the words *No entry.*

"Rats," Nancy said, tapping the monitor. She studied the screen for a moment. If REACH did have any trouble before, then maybe Mitch had changed the group's name. Quickly she brought up the Cults and Cult Leaders heading and typed in: Mitch Lebo.

The computer screen brought up a file on Mitch Lebo. His name occurred four times in an article about cults and campus groups in an old issue of *Psychological Profile* magazine.

"Gotcha," Nancy said, nodding her head. "Maybe you changed your group's name, Mr. Lebo, but you didn't change yours."

Nancy quickly logged on to the index of the Rock, Wilder's main library, to make sure they had an issue of the magazine.

"Yes!" Nancy shut down her computer, flung her pack over her shoulder, and raced off to the Rock.

"And you have *so* much to complain about," Eileen said good-naturedly. "I can barely keep a dry eye around you." Bess smiled as she listened to Eileen teasing Casey.

"That's not fair," Casey replied. "It's hard when the person you want to be with is on the opposite end of the country."

Lunchtime on Monday, Bess, Eileen, and Casey were hanging out in the living room of the Kappa house. "Poor Casey," Eileen said. "While the rest of us struggle to find a date, Casey Fontaine sits home alone and fans the coals of the barely burning romance she has going with her incredibly gorgeous, famous, long-distance Hollywood boyfriend. Truly a story to break your hearts, ladies and gentlemen."

"I hardly get to see him," Casey replied.

"Better for you anyway," Eileen replied. "That means you'll get good grades this semester."

"But wouldn't it be nice if I could see Charley all the time and *still* get good grades?" Casey said dreamily.

Bess sighed because she agreed. If only she didn't feel that having a boyfriend and doing well in school definitely did not go together.

"I feel if I take even one *tiny* little break from schoolwork," Bess began, "or put off even *one* homework assignment—"

"Whammo!" Eileen cried. "It's over."

Bess nodded vigorously. "Exactly."

"I'm sure your grade-hungry roommate doesn't help," Casey pointed out, leaning back against the couch and stretching her long legs. "Of course you should take school seriously. But this is college after all. You don't want to miss all the fun, do you?"

"Kappa is fun," Bess pointed out. "And so is being in the musical. That's another good week or so of fun right there."

"No." Casey waved her off. "Those are activities. I'm talking about real college fun and that always means—"

"Men!" Eileen chimed in. "I don't think that a few dates could hurt. Only I'm still waiting to get asked on even one. I know one guy I wouldn't mind getting to know better, but he seems to be interested in someone else." Eileen looked at Bess knowingly.

"Oh?" Casey perked up, and instantly she was sitting on the edge of the couch, staring at Bess. "Who are we discussing? Is this that gorgeous fellow who was pursuing you so passionately the other night?"

Immediately, Bess felt her face flame. Because now they were talking about Paul, and the truth was, Bess hadn't been able to get him out of her mind all afternoon.

"Well," Bess began hesitantly, "he *is* in Zeta."

"Oh, Bess," Casey cried. "You can't blame a whole fraternity for one guy's actions. I know you had an awful time with that jerk you met, but he's gone."

"It's history," Eileen agreed. "And that shouldn't be the only reason you won't date him."

"I know, I know," Bess murmured. Bess had already admitted to herself that the Zeta connection was an excuse. It seemed the easiest way not to think about how she felt about Paul.

"The truth is," Bess said, "I'm just nervous. I worry about school, and I feel like I'm just getting on top of it. Plus I'm involved in a lot of things I really care about right now. I don't want to give any of those up. And what if Paul is . . ." Bess faltered.

"The man of your dreams?" Eileen offered.

"So great you want to spend lots of time with him?" Casey added.

"Good reason not to pursue it," Eileen said seriously. "Perfect logic."

"Yep." Casey shrugged. "Case closed. He just has too much potential to be wonderful for you."

"Now you're making me sound like an idiot." Bess sighed. "Of course he's funny and great looking, and I can't believe he's still interested in me when I've been such a jerk. But I just want to make sure I'm not going to do something I'll regret. I'm feeling really good right now, that's all."

Immediately Casey leaned forward and put her arm around Bess. "Wait a minute," she explained. "Of course you're not an idiot. I do understand how you feel and it makes sense. We support you no matter what you decide."

"Thanks," Bess said, leaning her head on Casey's arm. Now all I have to do is decide, she told herself.

"What do you think?" Nancy asked, raising her voice so Bill could hear her over the late afternoon din in Java Joe's. She bent down to take a sip from her cappuccino. Bill was just finishing the photocopied *Psychological Profile* article Nancy had found at the library. He put the article on the table and shook his head. "What a slime."

Nancy nodded. "You bet he is. Did you read the part about how his special talent is getting female students to fall in love with him?"

Bill's lips tightened in anger. "Yes."

"What's amazing," Nancy went on, "is that according to the article, Weston would be the fifth college town he's been in in the last couple of years. He's just going around the country getting rich off troubled kids. Then, when he gets caught, he moves on. He's got money stashed in bank accounts all over the country. The guy's probably a millionaire."

Bill had balled up his hand into a fist. "Why can't they just throw him in jail?"

Nancy shrugged. "He's smart. None of the former REACH members has ever testified against him, and it's never been proven that what he's doing is illegal. Not yet, anyway."

"But how could anyone get hooked by this jerk?"

"Because REACH looks okay from the outside," Nancy said, swishing the last of her cappuccino in the bottom of her cup. "I have to admit, it looked good to me the other night. Those two REACH guys at the party were really nice. And some people, like Dawn, are so messed up emotionally, they don't even notice that REACH is weird." Nancy saw Bill nodding in agreement.

"And even Mitch, this morning, seemed like the kind of guy a girl would just love to bring home to show her parents. He seems squeaky clean, except—"

"Except that he's not," Bill finished the thought. He looked over his shoulder, worriedly scanning the quad outside the window. "We've got to show this article to Dawn."

Nancy shook her head. "I did some reading up on cults. People like Lebo are so good at their game that it usually takes a lot to get their followers to see reality. You have to overwhelm them with evidence."

"What's wrong?" Bill asked. "You look so worried."

"Unfortunately," Nancy replied slowly, "you also have to be very careful and patient. According to some of the stuff I read, Dawn is probably so vulnerable and scared right now that we could easily scare her away, right back into Mitch Lebo's arms—permanently."

"Great." Bill grimaced. He glanced jumpily at the window. "How long do you think it'll be before we hear anything from Stephanie?"

"I guess it depends on how long she can stand it." Nancy sighed. "I'm actually amazed she wasn't back first thing this morning."

"Well, I hope *she* can talk to Dawn," Bill said, cracking his knuckles for the tenth time. "Maybe if someone just talks to her, and convinces her to listen to us for just two minutes—"

I wish it were that easy, Nancy thought. She was suddenly filled with affection and admiration for Bill. He was a great guy. Yes, he was in love with Dawn, but he also was a great friend.

What about Jake? Nancy couldn't help wondering. Was he such a great friend right now?

"You're an incredibly sweet person," Nancy said quietly. "And a very good friend. Don't think Dawn doesn't appreciate it, even if it doesn't seem like it right now."

"Thanks for the pep talk, Nancy. But I feel so useless sitting here, drinking coffee."

"We just have to wait," Nancy argued, trying not to feel guilty about enjoying the cappuccino cup warming her hands. "We have to be patient. This is going to be really tricky."

Nancy scanned the crowd. As if she'd thought him up, suddenly, there was Jake across the room. He was sitting at a table of upperclassmen. Nancy watched him run his hands tiredly over his face, and she saw his wry grin as someone at the table made a joke that sent everyone else into gales of laughter. Then, as though he could feel her gaze, Jake turned and their eyes caught.

Nancy was overwhelmed with frustration from their conversation Saturday night. But she was sad he was still so far away from her.

In a second Jake made a move to rise. Nancy saw him push back his chair. But then, just as he was about to stand, she saw his eyes flicker, and she knew he was replaying their conversation, too. He sighed and dropped back into his chair, smiling sadly and refocusing on the group at his table.

Well, Nancy thought, trying to convince herself the hurt wasn't as bad as it seemed, I had to stand up for myself, didn't I?

"Will?" George called. Why doesn't he answer? she wondered, searching for the remote to the TV. If she didn't change the channel within ninety seconds, she'd go crazy watching more of this dumb show about lifeguards.

She slapped the couch in frustration. "Will, where are you?" she moaned miserably. With her ankle wrapped tightly and propped up on pillows, George was trying to rest as much as possible, hoping her foot would heal quickly. That meant, as Will kept pointing out, no jumping up and down for a drink or a snack or anything, including channel changing.

"Just call me," he'd promised. "I'm here to take care of you."

But where was he now when George finally needed him? "Where's the remote control when you need it," she complained.

George rolled over and grabbed one of the aluminum crutches leaning against a nearby chair.

"I have to change this channel," she murmured.

She held the crutch like a gun and aimed the rubber-tipped bottom at the little black box on top of the television and leaned forward.

"No more lifeguard babes in push-up bathing suits," George said through clenched teeth.

She leaned forward a little more. . . .

"George!" Will cried from behind her, just as she felt herself slipping. "What are you doing?"

"Ouch, my ankle," she moaned, and Will pushed her back onto the couch.

"I thought I told you not to get up," he said.

"Well, I called for you," George said defensively.

"I was on the phone to Oklahoma," Will explained, "talking to one of the officials at the Cherokee reservation. I heard you, but I couldn't come right away."

"Sorry. How's your art show proposal coming?" George asked.

"Okay," Will replied. "Only it's been hard trying to find the right people to give approval for the pieces I'd want to borrow for the show. I can see my phone bill this month is going to be terrible." Will perched himself on the couch next to her. "So what is it you want to watch?"

"I don't know." George shrugged listlessly. "I don't care."

"All right. Let's talk then," Will began. "You know you haven't said a single thing to me about how successful the Ten-K run was," he pointed out. "I heard from someone in my poli-sci class that you guys raised a ton of money for Earthworks. Aren't you pleased?"

"Whatever," George mumbled.

"George," Will said gently. "You're moping."

"I know." George sighed. "But I'm still so upset. I planned this for so long—the race and the parties. And I didn't get to enjoy any of it."

"Are you sure that's the only reason you're upset?" Will asked.

"Aside from not having much of a chance of making the track team in the spring? Yes," George replied. "That's all."

"Have you spoken to Pam yet?" Will wrapped his arms around her, and all of a sudden, George felt like weeping.

"You mean since she turned her back on me after the race?" George's voice wavered. "Since I went back to my room yesterday and found her note?"

"What note?" Will asked. "You didn't tell me about any note."

George quickly wiped a stray tear away and reached into her jeans. She unfolded a crumpled piece of paper, cleared her throat, and read.

"Since things between us are pretty awful right now. And since your support was so overwhelming, maybe I'll just do what you're doing: quit. Pam."

"What does that mean?" Will asked, perplexed.

"Who knows?" George sighed. "I don't know what she means by my 'support.' The only thing I can figure is that she's quitting our friendship. And I can't believe it. I mean, I know I accused her of causing the accident on purpose, but I was just angry. And upset. She knows I didn't mean it."

"I don't think she does," Will said, treading carefully.

"Well, I went to the race, didn't I?" George asked. "I know she saw me there. And I wanted her to do well. I just don't understand this. She's really holding a grudge."

"You don't think she feels you're the one holding the grudge?" Will asked gently.

"I'm the one who's still hurt," George said. *"I'm* the one who lost a shot at team tryouts, yet *she's* mad at *me."*

George shook her head. Some friend Pam turned out to be. When the chips were down, she just walked away. George's throat felt tight. And I was sure we'd be friends forever.

CHAPTER 10

Stephanie followed Dawn back into the REACH house and collapsed into one of the overstuffed couches.

She'd survived a full night of stupid chanting and group hugs, followed by a long day of handing out leaflets and putting up posters with Dawn and some of the other REACH freaks.

Now it was late Tuesday afternoon, and Stephanie's stomach was beginning to rumble.

Another little REACH tactic, she thought. They're trying to starve me into submission.

But Stephanie did understand how some people could get hooked on groups like this. Especially if they were the kind of losers who had no friends and no social life. A few all-nighters, followed by a few missed meals, were enough to disorient anyone. Automatic comatose zombies primed for brainwashing.

And what's with that nasty drink concoction? I swear there's something in it. But I can still party all night if I have to.

Stephanie scanned the REACH living room with all the well-pressed and smiling drones.

What bunk, she thought again, shaking her head as she watched Dawn leaning over to hug some mousy-haired girl nodding off against the wall. She doesn't even know the girl.

Yawning with boredom, Stephanie didn't think she'd learned anything particularly useful yet. Certainly nothing sinister.

Except that molasses drink stuff, Stephanie thought. Definitely something up with that.

But basically everyone just seems like an idiot. Just because some gorgeous guy says don't sleep, don't eat, give me your money, they all do it. Maybe they're getting what they deserve.

I'll give it until dinnertime, Stephanie decided. If the freaks want to starve me through another meal, that'll be it. Stephanie's stomach grumbled again, and she almost laughed. Funny how appealing even dorm food seemed after minor starvation. Maybe everyone on campus should try it.

It was late afternoon, and Paul Cody was sitting on one of the stone benches scattered around campus. He was trying to figure out a way to get through Bess Marvin's defenses.

I feel like a high school kid, he thought to himself. I've never felt this way—about anyone.

"Until Bess," he muttered.

He wasn't sure how much more rejection he

could take. He'd told her everything that he was feeling.

"Maybe that's the problem," he thought aloud. "I said too much and scared her away. It's just that she's so busy all the time, I feel rushed every time I see her."

The truth was, there'd been no time to hang out together to see if Bess's feelings were the same. He wanted to get to know her, take her out to dinner, to the movies. Get her alone for just a little while, to hold her hand and talk.

Paul wanted to yell, "She's making me insane!"

Just then the front doors of a building across the lawn opened, and a flood of students spilled out in an array of jackets and sweaters. Paul saw a vaguely familiar face in the crowd and paused. Who was that guy in the windbreaker? Where have I seen him?

Paul snapped his fingers. "That's it! This may be desperate, but these are desperate times."

"Hey!" Paul called out, racing across the lawn to the blond guy in the red windbreaker.

The guy paused and waited as Paul jogged the rest of the way to him.

"Isn't your . . ."—Paul struggled to speak while catching his breath—"name—Brian? I saw you the other day at the race registration tables. We weren't introduced. You and Bess were on your way to the library."

Brian nodded. "Paul, right? You were the one trying to entice my study partner to bag out on me."

Paul grinned. "But the library won out over my lowly offer of a date. Anyway, I know it's strange of me to ask you this, but I'm getting desperate."

Brian eyed him. "Go on. Sounds interesting."

"I sort of wanted to know, are you and Bess? What I mean is, are you guys . . . ?'"

Brian laughed. "Are we going out?"

Paul managed a crooked smile. "Yes."

"Well, if it means anything to you," Brian replied, "the answer is a decided no. We're just good friends."

"Great," Paul said, obviously relieved.

"Okay. Let me guess," Brian said. "You're glad Bess and I aren't going out because *you* want to go out with her?"

"Bingo," Paul said shyly. "But I can't get anywhere. I'm totally crazy about her. She's wonderful. Attractive. Funny."

"You're right about all that," Brian agreed.

"But every time I tell her that, she looks at me like I'm crazy. I was kind of hoping that honesty would help me stand out from the rest of the crowd," Paul continued. "So far, it seems to have been a total turnoff."

Brian stared at him. "You're really serious about her?"

"As serious as I can get, considering she'll hardly talk to me," Paul replied. "I just can't figure her out. I'd like to believe it's because she's really as busy as she says. I'd even be happy for ten minutes of her time if I could get them."

Brian crossed his arms over his chest, considering. He looked Paul up and down. Finally he nodded.

"Okay," he said quickly. "I don't know if I should do this, but you seem pretty sincere, and you're a nice guy. You really want to show Bess that you're interested?"

Paul nodded enthusiastically.

"I have an idea. Bess is a woman with a fun sense of humor. She'd want that in a guy she dates, too. Are you willing to show her you have one?" Brian asked mischievously.

"Sure," Paul answered.

Brian checked his watch. "The *Grease!* performance ends at ten-thirty tonight. Meet me," Brian said, "right here at ten-forty."

"Ten-forty," Paul repeated, a flicker of excitement and hope curling in his stomach as he watched Brian walk away.

Then Brian stopped and turned around. "Can you sing?" he called out, almost as an afterthought.

"Not at all," Paul yelled back.

"Perfect!" Brian laughed. "Even better than perfect!"

Jake leaned back and put his feet up on his desk. His chair squeaked and groaned as he shifted.

"You ever going to fix that thing, Collins?" someone called out from the other side of the *Wilder Times* office.

"Nah," he mumbled, rocking back and forth in the squeaky chair. "Helps me think."

Right now, he had a lot to think about, and her name was Nancy Drew.

"What kind of guy does she think I am?" Jake murmured to himself, recalling her anger about her promotion. Anyone else would have been glad to know they had someone in their corner.

What he wanted to do was run over to Nancy's dorm, drag her away somewhere where they wouldn't be interrupted, and calm her once and for all about this whole promotion business.

He hadn't gotten the promotion for her. He wouldn't have done that for anybody, no matter how great her legs were. And Nancy's legs were incredible.

Of course he hadn't hesitated to add his two cents about Nancy's terrific writing, when Gail first brought it up, but he hadn't even suggested the promotion.

The problem now was that Nancy didn't believe him. How could he find a way to make her believe the truth?

Jake rubbed his hand over his eyes and groaned.

There was nothing he could do but wait.

She's the one who misunderstood you, hotshot, Jake reminded himself. Which meant she was the one who had to make it right.

"I can be just as stubborn as you, Ms. Drew," Jake muttered, hoping it was true as he said it. Because he'd be seeing her the next day at the staff meeting. And if she didn't have something to say to him by then, he might end up eating those words.

*   *   *

Nancy was rearranging piles of papers, letters, even paper clips at her desk. Anything to avoid remembering the expression in Jake's eyes when she saw him yesterday in Java Joe's. How did such good news turn into such a mess? Nancy wondered.

Frustrated, she opened her Western Civ book and tried to read the chapter they'd been assigned. But she just couldn't concentrate.

"Well, well, well," a voice drawled from the doorway. "I'm suffering away with a crowd of paranoid freaks, and you're catching up on your homework? You're such a good girl, Nancy Drew."

"Stephanie!" Nancy cried, slamming her book shut. "You're back!"

Stephanie rolled her eyes. "With Ms. Steiger."

Nancy quickly got on her feet. "Where?"

Stephanie lowered her voice to a whisper. "She's in her room. We're supposed to be picking up our clothes, *permanently*—"

"Permanently?"

"As ordered by His Royal Supreme Commander Mr. Mitch," Stephanie went on. "Unfortunately, Dawn's as committed to that bunch of wackos as ever."

"Nancy?" It was Dawn's voice.

When Dawn appeared in the doorway, Nancy had to force herself to smile. She looked awful, even paler than before. Her hair was dirty, and her eyes were unfocused, as if she'd been up for days.

"How are you?" Nancy asked.

Dawn smiled wearily. "Never been better." She turned to Stephanie. "Mitch said to come right back."

Have to work quick, Nancy told herself. "Um, there's something I want to show you," she said. "Something I found."

She handed Dawn the copy of the article. As Dawn read the page, her hand began to shake.

She stared at Nancy bleary-eyed. "What is this?" she asked accusingly.

Nancy remembered that she had to be gentle. She couldn't attack her. She had to get Dawn to see for herself what REACH was all about. "What do you think it is?"

Her eyes narrowing, Dawn crumpled the page in her hand and dropped it to the floor. "It's a lie," she snapped. "That's what it is. You're just jealous of my happiness with REACH. That's how Mitch said everyone would be. You're not really concerned about *me*. Stephanie, don't listen to her lies!"

"When was the last time you saw yourself in the mirror, Dawn?" Nancy asked calmly.

Dawn shrugged and gazed out the window. "We don't have any mirrors at the REACH house."

Nancy took a step toward Dawn. Dawn tensed. "I'm not going to hurt you," Nancy assured her. "Just look. That's all I'm asking."

As she turned Dawn by the shoulders toward the mirror, Nancy heard her give a little gasp of surprise. A stricken expression came over Dawn's face as she touched her thin neck, her hollowed cheeks, her dry, tangled hair. Then she looked away. "I just lost a little weight," she said.

"Dawn, you look terrible. Not like yourself at all," said Nancy.

Dawn stiffened. "I'm going back. *Now,*" she declared. "Coming, Stephanie?"

Stephanie shrugged helplessly at Nancy. "I'll be right there, Dawn. Just let me get my clothes."

"I'll meet you downstairs," Dawn said. She glared at Nancy. "And don't talk to her. She doesn't know what's good for us."

"You got it, kiddo," Stephanie said. "Just give me a sec."

Dawn whirled around and stalked out of the room.

As she heard the suite door slam shut, Nancy shook her head. Her heart sank, and she lowered herself into her chair.

"Wow," she said, stunned. "She's in really deep."

"I told you she was," Stephanie insisted. "I can't tell you what a drag this has been."

She lounged in the doorway and hungrily lit a cigarette. "Oh, I've been *dying* for one of these. I'm beginning to think you're all wasting your time. Dawn's a total flake. If she can't see through all that bunk she deserves what she gets."

"She's not a flake! And no one deserves to be used like that," Nancy replied, still jolted by what she'd just seen.

Stephanie blew a stream of smoke past Nancy's face. Nancy waved her hand, coughing.

"Stephanie, do you mind?"

Rolling her eyes, Stephanie put out the cigarette against the bottom of her shoe. "You guys are all so antismoking—it's boring," she muttered. "Anyway, if I didn't want to see that creep Mitch get caught so much, I'd leave right now," Stephanie admitted. "Those people are a bunch of kooks."

"Has he asked you for anything yet?" Nancy asked. "I mean, does he ask right out in the open?"

Stephanie nodded. "He asked me this morning. After we'd all been up all night. I guess I was supposed to be too sleepy to think straight." Stephanie smiled wryly. "I was commended for studying, but I won't really get anywhere until I embrace the first precept."

"Which is?"

"Releasing my hold on material wealth," Stephanie intoned.

"Give up your money," Nancy said, nodding. "What a jerk."

Stephanie braced herself against the door and yawned.

Nancy raised her eyes. "Tired?"

Stephanie arched her eyebrows. "A little—I guess. I'm pretty sure now that that molasses and lemon stuff they make us drink is doped."

Nancy picked up the balled-up article and pried it apart again. "This said the authorities suspected that!" she said excitedly. "But they could never get evidence. Everyone was too afraid of him to testify."

Stephanie eyed the paper in Nancy's hands. "What is that thing anyway? It must be good. It really made Dawn mad."

"This isn't the first time Mr. Lebo has visited a college campus," Nancy said. "Take a look."

Stephanie read quickly. "Oh yeah, this guy's smooth all right. Very studied. He and his *close* followers know just the right buttons to push." She looked up. "Mitch and his aides show up in the morning, go for the collection, and then leave." She waved the article. "But why don't you just show this to everyone and let them read for themselves what a slime he is?"

Nancy told her what she'd found out about the dangers of "rescuing" people from cults. "You saw how Dawn reacted," she said. "But wait a second. He doesn't live there? Isn't that his house?"

"He says he's got some cheap dive on the other side of town. He needs to be alone to concentrate on his writings or something like that. He keeps it real private. Most of the other REACH members aren't allowed to go there."

"Another place," Nancy said thoughtfully. Her mind was racing. "Tell me more about the REACH house."

Stephanie shrugged. "It's like living inside a coffin with all those zombies wandering around with their fake little smiles. But," she pointed out, "it is clean and neat. And there's more than enough room for him to live there if he didn't need his 'privacy.' Then again, if I were him, I'd try to spend as little time with those loonies as possible," Stephanie said, arching her brows. "A few of them do live with him, though. His aides. They're the inner circle. The real converts."

Or the ones who know the real Mitch? Nancy thought. After all, what's so mysterious about a cheap apartment? Why does he have to be so private?

Unless he didn't want anyone else to see the way he lived because he wasn't in a cheap apartment.

A rich guy like that living in a dive? Nancy thought. No way.

Nancy checked her watch. "What time does he usually leave?"

"Seven," Stephanie replied, checking her own watch. "Just before the nondinner."

"You must be starving," Nancy said.

Stephanie winked. "I'm way ahead of them. They think I'm getting some clothes. But I'm making a pit stop for a pizza before I go back. That is, if I *have* to?"

Nancy was amazed Stephanie was even taking the time to help. "Could you stand it one more night? Just to keep an eye on Dawn?"

"Okay," Stephanie replied. "I'll make sure she doesn't sign over her house or anything. Don't worry about me, of course."

"Stephanie, I'll *never* worry about you," Nancy assured her with a laugh.

Stephanie turned and went into her room for a change of clothes, and Nancy reached for the phone. She wanted to make sure Bill was free that night. She had a feeling about Mitch's "dive" apartment.

"An article might not be enough to convince Dawn," she thought aloud. "But what about hard evidence?"

I can't believe I'm actually cracking a book, Bess thought to herself as she lay facedown on her bed with her biology textbook under her nose. I'm so exhausted I can't even focus.

That night's performance of *Grease!* had gone great. It seemed to Bess that the show had gotten better and better with every performance. Probably it just seemed that way because after so many performances, it finally felt natural.

Bess loved being in the musical, but it was also really tiring. Bess had to admit she'd be happy when it was over. Only a few more performances to go. It was amazing how even the fun stuff seemed like work after a while.

Bess rolled over on her back and tried to muffle an enormous yawn with her arm.

"Excuse me," came the icy cold voice across the room. "If studying is so overwhelming for your feeble brain, please don't overtax yourself."

Bess turned to glare at her roommate. Even though it was after eleven at night, Leslie was sitting up at her desk, fully awake and fully clothed. For all she knew, it could be two in the afternoon.

"The excessive yawning and random page-flipping is really distracting," Leslie snapped. "Some of us are serious about our work. It's difficult to be productive with disruptive unfiltered noises all over the place."

Bess didn't even bother to respond. The comments were actually pretty tame for Leslie. If I had anywhere else to go, Bess thought, I'd be there. The room was deadly silent, but Bess knew Leslie would find something to complain about. Bess thought about all the little disturbing noises she'd probably make just getting ready for bed. She sighed again.

"Excuse me," Leslie said through clenched teeth.

Bess was about to say something when she heard her name called from outside the open window.

"What the—" Leslie began.

"BESS!"

Bess's eyes popped open in surprise. Her name was being called from below.

"BESS! BESS ARE YOU THERE?"

Bess ran to the window. It took her a moment to adjust her eyes to the gloominess outside, but then she made out two figures down below on Jamison's lawn.

"Who's there," Bess called out in a loud whisper. "Be quiet, I'm studying."

"WE HAVE A SURPRISE FOR YOU!" the voice cried.

"Bess!" Leslie said sharply, her hands on her hips. "Do you know who that is out there? Did you plan this? Are you doing this on purpose just to bug me?"

"Oh, shut up!" Bess cried, turning her back

on her angry roommate and staring back out the window. This was much more interesting.

"THIS IS FOR YOU, BESS!" the voice called out, a little less sure of itself now.

Wait a second, she thought. I know that voice.

Bess leaned out farther and tried to get a better look at who was outside. "Brian!" she called. "Is that you?"

"The one and only!" he screamed back.

"Who's that with you?" Bess yelled, laughing.

"Listen," Brian replied.

Bess watched as Brian huddled with someone. Suddenly the second figure turned around and started singing: " 'IF I CAN'T HAVE YOU, I DON'T WANT NOBODY, BABY . . .' "

It was Paul! Bess realized. She felt herself start to blush. She saw lights popping on at most of the other windows. Heads poked out into the darkness.

"What *is* that?" someone screamed.

" 'IF I CAN'T HAVE YOU, I DON'T WANT NOBODY, BABY . . .' "

The voice cracked and wavered off-key.

"I can't believe this," Bess said, laughing. "He's such a goof. I think I'm going to die."

She collapsed against the window sill as she listened to Paul struggle his way through an entire verse of the song.

" 'IF I CAN'T HAVE YOU,' " Paul went on gamely.

Somehow, it was one of the sweetest sounds Bess had ever heard. Paul was making a complete fool of himself—and he was doing it all for her.

"I'm calling the campus police!" someone called out from the second floor.

"BESS!" Paul called up to her. "DO YOU THINK WE COULD..."

Just then Leslie pulled Bess from the window and slammed it closed.

"That's it!" Leslie cried. "I can't spend all night listening to that garbage." Leslie nervously arranged herself back at her desk.

Bess didn't even bother to reply. She was a little disappointed that she hadn't heard the rest of Paul's question because she had a feeling she knew what her answer would have been. I think we could, she might have said. I think we could.

Chapter 11

The REACH house glowed in the moonlight. Through a downstairs window of the house, Nancy could just make out Dawn sitting at a table, bent over a book.

"It looks like everyone's studying," Bill said, shaking his head. "I can't believe that people—smart people—would actually fall for that junk."

"You'd be surprised what people will fall for if they're desperate enough," Nancy replied sadly.

She and Bill were sitting in Nancy's Mustang, across the street from the house. She'd parked the car a house away, near a broken street lamp, so they couldn't be seen.

"That's Mitch," Nancy said, pointing.

Mitch's imposing figure was crossing one window, then another. He was wearing khakis and a long-sleeved denim shirt rolled up to the elbows.

"I can see why everyone's so attracted to him," Bill said.

"No kidding," Nancy agreed. "And don't think he doesn't know it. He has using his looks to get what he wants down to a science."

Suddenly the big front door swung open, and Mitch filled the doorway as he waved goodbye to his converts.

"Get down!" Nancy whispered, and she and Bill sank low in the Mustang's bucket seats.

Nancy's eyes followed Mitch as he led three others to a small, inexpensive sedan. After the car pulled away, she waited five seconds before taking off after it.

Nancy tailed the car to an indoor parking garage in town. Nancy pulled her car over at the curb as Mitch's car went in through the gates.

"We can't follow them in there," Bill said dejectedly.

"We won't have to," Nancy replied, keeping her eyes glued to the gate.

Bill looked at her. "What do you mean?"

"If my hunch is right—"

In less than a minute, the gate opened, and another car pulled through with Mitch at the wheel, and the others in the front and back. Nancy restarted her engine.

"See what I mean?"

"I'm glad *someone* knows what she's doing," Bill said admiringly. "Driver, follow that car!"

"And what a car it is," Nancy said, whistling.

Mitch had left the parking garage in a huge, elegant luxury car, built for comfort and looks.

"Why aren't I surprised?" Bill said dryly.

"Not a penny spared," Nancy mused. "Somehow, I didn't think Mitch was the type for ugly compact cars. Or old clothes, for that matter. I bet that we haven't seen the last of his transformations."

Nancy eased back a car or two as they drove. Mitch's new car had distinctive taillights, so Nancy wasn't worried about losing him. They followed the car to the outskirts of Weston, then onto the four-lane road that headed toward Chicago.

Bill sank deep into his seat. "I have a feeling it's going to be a long night."

Peering over her knuckles on the steering wheel, Nancy nodded.

A half hour later, Nancy was following Mitch off an exit ramp and through the streets of an exclusive community. She couldn't even see most of the houses over the walls and hedges and iron gates.

Mitch slowed and pulled into a long, winding driveway. Nancy stopped at the curb. The house at the top of the drive was a huge, stone mansion.

Bill gasped. "The lawn's big enough for a football field."

Nancy was seething. "I'm sure he has one out back. Next to the tennis courts."

Bill was shaking his head. "So much for the REACH credo of giving up all your worldly possessions."

"The hypocrite," Nancy fumed, her voice laced with accusation. A half hour away, in Weston, a dozen poor Wilder students were starving themselves, giving over their last dimes—and all for a guy who drove home in his fancy car to his immense estate in the country.

Bill nodded toward the house. "Here they come again."

Nancy could see them filing out of the front door. Mitch's denim shirt and old pants were gone. Now he wore a linen blazer and linen pants, and a shirt that shimmered, probably made of silk. The others were just as well dressed.

They returned to the car and pulled out of the driveway. Nancy followed them to a beautiful restaurant. Through the large picture windows, Nancy could see inside. The lights were low, the tables candlelit, and the waiters had linen cloths draped over their arms.

"I bet you can't get a burger and fries in there," Nancy said dryly.

As Mitch and company were seated at a large, round table and handed menus, Nancy and Bill sagged in their car seats and sighed. Nancy was so angry, her knuckles on the wheel went white.

"You've got to hand it to him," Bill said, defeated. "He's an incredibly intelligent guy."

Nancy gritted her teeth. *"Clever,"* she corrected him. *"Intelligent* people wouldn't steal from the poor or take advantage of the weak."

But not clever enough, she thought. Not clever enough.

"Come on, Brian," Bess said as she and Brian stood on the little stage of the Attic, the small theater space above Java Joe's that the drama department used for small class productions and workshops. Though it was early Wednesday morning, in the Attic it could have been any time of the day or night. It was a cozy, windowless place where time had no meaning.

Brian cleared his throat and lifted the script. He cringed. "I just can't say these lines," Brian complained. "They're just too—"

"Awful, I know," Bess agreed. "But you're directing it in class next week, don't forget."

Brian slid down to the edge of the stage. "Let's talk instead," he said excitedly.

Bess perked up. She'd like nothing better. She was developing a special camaraderie with Brian that was totally new to her: a man who wasn't interested in her romantically, but was interested in her as a friend.

"So what do you want to talk about?" Bess asked.

"How'd you like Paul's little serenade?"

Bess laughed and just shrugged.

Inwardly, she thought Paul was great and cute and funny, too.

Brian leveled his I-want-to-know-and-I-want-to-know-now look. "Why don't you want to talk about him?"

Bess took a big breath. "Because if I do, that means he'll be real, and I'll have to deal with it, and I don't want to deal with it because I don't have the time right now, because I have homework and Kappa, and Nancy and George, and *Grease!* performances, and I have to have time to eat and sleep. There, did I cover it all?"

Brian nodded. "I guess you did." He pointed at the bench Bess was sitting on. "Hand me my book bag?"

Bess handed it over. Brian dug deep into it and brought out a small gift-wrapped package. "Here, for you," he said. "Not that you deserve it," he added under his breath.

"I heard that," Bess grumbled, taking the package. She eyed it. "What is this, Bri?"

Brian shrugged. "It's not from me."

Bess opened the card. It said, simply, "Paul." She gulped.

"There, you're blushing already," Brian said, pointing at her face.

"I am not," Bess replied.

"Just open the package," Brian commanded.

Bess tore at the paper. It was a small, natural leather softbound book. Embossed on the cover in red, it said, "A Busy Woman's Datebook." Bess turned it over and fanned the pages.

"It's a calendar," she said. "Wait, there's stuff written in it already."

Here and there, every few days or so, there were ten-minute slots inked in. They all read, "Ten minutes with Paul."

Bess was shaking her head, unable to keep herself from grinning. "He's really funny."

"He's also really crazy about you," Brian pointed out. "Say, what's that?" He pointed at that day's page. "Well, what do you know, you have a ten-minute date with Paul *tonight* after the show. Right downstairs in Java Joe's, too!" Brian slapped his knee. "What a coincidence."

Bess raised her eyes to the darkened ceiling and sighed. Face it, Marvin, she said to herself, Paul is too good to ignore. That decision you've been putting off seems to have already been made. . . .

"But how are we going to get to Dawn now?" Bill asked as he and Nancy pulled up to the REACH house in Nancy's Mustang. "We can't just walk up to the door and say, 'Hi. We're here to steal Dawn back.' "

"But that's the point," Nancy replied, "we don't want to steal her back. That's what *they* would do. We just want to convince her what a farce REACH is."

Nancy drummed her fingers on the wheel, thinking. "Not that she believed me the last time," she said.

The front door of the house opened and out stepped Stephanie, stretching and shaking her head.

"There's Steph—" Nancy said. "And, boy, does she look bummed."

"Wouldn't you? Wait, there's Dawn."

Dawn came out right behind Stephanie, blinking at the morning sky.

Nancy held her breath, praying they'd be alone. They started walking down the steps, toward the street. Stephanie was dragging a shopping cart.

"Excellent," Nancy whispered. "They're going shopping."

Then Stephanie noticed Nancy's car and

started to point, but Nancy waved her to keep going. "We'll wait until they're out of sight of the house," Nancy said.

"Doesn't Dawn know what kind of car you drive?" Bill asked.

"Look," Nancy said. "She's totally out of it."

Dawn was even more zombielike, walking with unstable, baby steps with her head down.

When they turned the corner, Nancy pulled away from the curb and slowly drove up beside them. "Dawn!" she called.

Dawn was so spaced out, she didn't seem to recognize Nancy.

"It's Nancy and Bill," Stephanie prodded her. Then she stuck her head in the passenger's side window. "I'm *so* glad you guys are here. Pop the trunk and I'll throw this stupid cart in."

After Stephanie had put the shopping cart in the trunk, Bill slid his seat forward so she could climb into the backseat.

Dawn didn't move.

"Don't you want a lift?" Nancy asked.

"She's totally zoned out," Stephanie whispered.

"Mitch said we shouldn't take rides. Especially from nonbelievers," Dawn said.

"But we're your friends!" Bill said.

"That's what Mitch said you'd say. Besides, Nancy wasn't my friend yesterday."

"Dawn, they're just giving us a lift to the store," Stephanie called to her. "You can trust me. Just to the store and back."

Dawn warily looked around, then got in the

car. The second she closed her door, Nancy pulled away.

"Thank you, thank you, thank you," Stephanie said.

Nancy drove through town toward the highway.

"This isn't the way to the store. We have to pick up more lemons and molasses," Dawn said.

In the rearview mirror, Nancy watched Dawn. "Have you ever been to Mitch's house?"

Dawn shook her head. "He needs the time to be alone so he can work on his writings for REACH. We respect his space. He has a simple place somewhere on the edge of town. Where are you taking me?"

"We want you to see who Mitch *really* is," Bill said.

Dawn seemed near tears. "We won't be there when he arrives at REACH house. He'll be so mad. Take me back—*please,*" she begged.

"We will, Dawn," Nancy said. "Soon."

She drove quickly. Every few minutes Dawn complained about not being back on time, but Nancy kept driving. She pulled off the exit and wound through the exclusive town toward Mitch's house. "Nice houses, huh, Dawn?" she asked.

Dawn didn't reply.

Nancy pulled up to the front of Mitch's mansion.

"Home sweet home," Bill said sarcastically.

"This is where Mitch really lives," Nancy said.

Dawn laughed. "What are you talking about?"

Then the front door opened, and Mitch and his followers stepped out. Nancy could hear Dawn gasp.

"Seen enough now?" Stephanie asked. "Wasn't it enough that Mitch was written up in a national magazine as a low-down dirty liar. Now look at that!"

Dawn was shaking her head. "There must be some mistake." She motioned at the luxury car in the driveway. "That's not his!"

"Just wait," Nancy said, pulling away and heading back toward Weston and the parking garage where Mitch switched cars. "Just wait and see."

Dawn started to yell. "I don't believe you! This is just what Mitch predicted. You'd try to steal me away." Dawn started to cry. "He makes me so happy. He loves me."

Upset for her friend, and upset that she might have already lost her, a saddened Nancy grimly drove on.

I don't get it, Dawn thought as she staggered back into the REACH house. That beautiful mansion Mitch came out of, that huge car he switched out of. And that restaurant Nancy and Bill said they saw him in. Mitch eats only simple food, like us. And that article: four towns in two years? What did that mean?

"Dawn, where have you been?" Mitch asked, stepping out of his office. "We've all been here waiting for you. And where's Stephanie?"

We've been waiting? Dawn repeated in her

foggy brain. But you got here just before I did. Didn't you?

Dawn stepped into his office and held the door for support. "I don't know," she started to say, but she was so tired she was having trouble forming complete thoughts. "My friends—"

Mitch shot to his feet. "I thought so."

"Mitch, I don't understand," Dawn said beseechingly. "They took me to a big expensive house, and I saw you come out of it. Then you got into this huge car."

Mitch wiped away his sour expression and, grinning, took Dawn's face in his hands. "Dawn, dear. You're so beautiful. That wasn't *my* house." Laughing, he closed the office door. "How could I possibly live in disgusting wealth? You know I live across town, in a little run-down apartment."

Dawn squinted through her fog. "But I saw you."

"But of course you saw me! Don't you believe your eyes? Open your eyes, Dawn, and see clearly for the first time in your life! I *was* in that house, but I was meeting with a wealthy patron of ours, begging him for the small amount he donates to keep our cause afloat."

"You were? But—but how would Nancy know where he lived?"

"Forget Nancy," Mitch said quickly. "She's blind to the truth, *our* truth. Now come here, I want to show you something."

Mitch took her by the hand and led her into his chair. "See how little money we have?" Dawn looked at the bank deposit slip on the desk. It said, REACH, Inc. The deposit amount was $34.06, and the balance read, $241.84.

"You see?" Mitch said gently, stroking Dawn's hair. "How could I afford a spectacular house like that and a fancy car, with $241.84? Everything I have, I give to you. Everything you have, you give to me. Together, we have just enough to live. That's our cause. That's our journey."

Dawn started to cry. She was so mad she could shout. She could kill Nancy for humiliating her! Of course Mitch was telling the truth. He couldn't lie if he tried!

"Mitch, I'm so sorry. I can't believe I didn't trust you. My friends had me so confused."

"Don't be hurt," Mitch said, "or mad at them. That's the way others live. We live for forgiveness. Don't you see that their anger is self-love, just as I said? They can't understand why you don't want what they want, Dawn. They're jealous that they aren't enough for you. But *we're* your friends. Your *only* friends. Now sit there. I'll bring you a tissue and something to relax you. You look like you could use a nice, long sleep. Wouldn't you like that?"

"Yes," Dawn said, her speech slurred, her hands and feet numb with fatigue. She laid her head on the desk. "I'm tired, so tired."

CHAPTER 12

Nancy was walking across the quad in a daze. Tired from all the events of the last two days and worried about Dawn, she was heading to the *Wilder Times* building for the Wednesday morning staff meeting.

After she entered the building, Nancy paused outside the staff room. She felt more jumpy than before because she knew that Jake was probably already inside. He was usually early for staff meetings. At these meetings Gail gave out assignments, and all the reporters would update everyone on the stories they were working on.

Nancy could picture Jake, standing and leaning against the wall in a corner of the room. Her stomach clenched as she took a step forward. What would it be like to see him?

Nancy was almost disappointed to realize there would be no big scene to worry about. She wanted to get it over with. But the staff room was packed, and everyone was talking and laughing. Nancy glanced around and saw that Jake was in conversation with another senior reporter on the paper.

Nancy pushed down the pang of jealousy she felt when she saw that the other reporter was an attractive dark-haired woman who wrote all the arts reviews.

"Hey, Nancy, congratulations!"

Nancy turned to the sports page editor, who was giving her the thumbs-up sign.

"Yeah, we heard you made full reporter," another senior staffer said, smiling.

"Thanks," Nancy replied, blushing as she dropped into an open seat. On Monday Gail had tacked up a notice about Nancy's promotion, but this was the first day since then that Nancy was seeing most of the staff. A few first-year staffers looked over and smiled at her, a mixture of shy support and envy in their eyes.

"But you're still a regular staffer," Gail reminded her, "so as a treat let me start with you, Drew. Next week I want you to give me something on the fiftieth reunion of the Class of '45 Ladies Singing Group. They're performing in the chapel on Sunday. Try to make it snappy."

Nancy's jaw dropped. "Wow, Gail, thanks a lot."

All around her, the room broke into laughter.

If Gail was pressured into giving me the promotion in the first place, Nancy thought to herself, maybe she feels she has to give me the worst assignment just to knock me back down to size.

Ten minutes later Gail had made it through all the assignments. As the meeting broke up, Nancy lingered, hoping she might have a chance to speak with Jake. She couldn't stand feeling that they were strangers, even if he was the one who got her her promotion.

Nancy sighed. Face it, Drew, she told herself. You miss the big jerk.

"Nancy?" Gail put her hand on Nancy's arm and snapped her from her reverie. "Do you have anything you want to run by me?"

"Excuse me?" Nancy said, startled. "What do you mean?"

Gail gave Nancy a funny look and pursed her lips. "I told you Friday that you could pursue your own leads with my approval. I thought for sure you already had a list of ideas for articles."

"Oh, right," Nancy said. "Ideas."

"Did you think they were just going to fall in your lap?" Gail asked incredulously.

"No, of course not," Nancy replied quickly. She couldn't admit to Gail that she'd been sidetracked by trouble with her boyfriend, and she couldn't use her missing R.A. as an excuse, or could she? If REACH was really what she and Bill had begun to suspect, it could be a very important story.

"Actually," Nancy began, "I do have something I'm looking into. But I just want to get a few more facts before I bring it to you."

At the magic word *facts*, Gail smiled. "Okay,

but don't let it sit too long," Gail warned. "I thought you were hungry for this. That's why I made the decision I did. I hope I wasn't wrong."

"Don't worry, Gail," a voice spoke up from behind them. Nancy turned to see Jake leaning in the doorway. Immediately her heart started beating faster.

"You made a good decision," Jake continued. "You always do." Finally, he let his eyes rest on Nancy. "I'm sure she won't disappoint you."

Before Nancy could speak or even smile, Jake was gone. Nancy hugged her books to her chest, feeling more alone than ever. She hadn't needed words to know what Jake would have said if he'd stayed. I'm sure she won't disappoint you, he'd said. Even if she's disappointed me.

As Mitch walked out of the office, Dawn's tears became a flood. She scanned the room for something she could use to blow her nose. She tugged open the desk drawer. But inside the drawer were only pens and pencils, rubber bands—and a stack of papers that looked suspiciously like the deposit slip Mitch had just shown her.

Same bank, Dawn noticed, but different name: instead of REACH, Inc., the top slip said simply Mitch Lebo. And instead of a balance of $241.84, this account had a balance of $52,485.21!

Dawn held her breath. Unblinking, she stared at the account balance. Then, glancing quickly over her shoulder, she riffled through the stack of slips. Mitch had been depositing money every

Monday morning for months. The balance was going up and up! The same time he deposited a few dollars in the REACH account, he'd deposited hundreds, sometimes thousands, in his personal account!

At first Dawn tried to convince herself there was a logical explanation for this, just like Mitch's for the house and the car. But the more she looked at the different deposit slips, the more everything Nancy and Bill had been trying to tell her made sense. Mitch was a liar.

Dawn shut the drawer just as the office door opened. Mitch returned with a box of tissues and a glass of water, smiling serenely. Just looking at him made Dawn want to be sick.

But I have to look at him, Dawn commanded herself. He mustn't realize I know. I'm not sure what he'd do. . . .

"I'm okay now," she managed to say. "Thank you, Mitch. Let me go do that shopping. We still need molasses and lemons."

Mitch stared at her intensely. "Can you handle it? Are you sure you see the truth clearly now?"

Somehow, Dawn summoned the strength to look him in the eye. "As clear as day."

"Here, take these," Mitch said, opening his hand. Two of the so-called herbal pills lay in his palm. "By the time you get back, you'll be ready for your nap."

Dawn gulped. What do I do?

She had no choice. She took the pills and the glass of water.

"Now swallow them," Mitch said.

"Thank you," Dawn forced herself to say. She opened her mouth, squeezed her eyes shut, and tucked the pills under her tongue as she swallowed some water.

I can't stay out of my dorm room forever, George thought as she hobbled toward her door. There's no room for me to live at Will and Andy's.

Staring at the line of light under the door, she knew Pam was inside. She felt jittery and nervous.

What are you nervous about? she asked herself. *You're* the one who got hurt. *You're* the one who went to cheer her on at the race and got zero thanks for it.

Taking a big breath, she opened the door. On her way in, she caught one of the crutches on the door and almost fell, catching herself at the last second on her good foot and hopping over to her bed.

Pam was lying on her back on her bed, staring at the ceiling. "You okay?" she murmured.

George shrugged and sat on her bed. She fiddled with her crutch and fluffed her pillow. Pam cleared her throat, as if she was getting ready to speak, but nothing came out.

George couldn't take the silence anymore. It was worse than an argument. They were going to have it out or forget it.

"Great note," George said. "I really didn't know what you were talking about, but if you want to dump this friendship, then say so."

Pam sighed sadly. "For some reason, when I saw you at the race, I thought you were actually there to cheer me on. But obviously you just showed up to see how badly I'd do."

"What do you mean?"

"You didn't say anything. You didn't cheer. You didn't even smile."

George shook her head. "I was watching you the whole time, thinking to myself, 'Don't quit, don't quit.' "

"Really? 'Don't quit'?" Pam repeated hopefully.

"Yeah, as in keep going, do well, etc." George leveled a pseudo-mean glare at her. "But I was too embarrassed at what I said to you to cheer out loud. I was just feeling sorry for myself and being mad at myself."

The beginnings of a smile flickered in the corners of Pam's mouth. "Oh."

"Don't 'oh' me," George said. "And another thing. Considering that your best competition wasn't even in the race—"

"That would be you?" Pam interrupted.

"That would be me," George continued. "Considering I wasn't running, it's totally unacceptable that my roommate, you, Pam, finished as badly as you did. You *should* have won."

"Well, if *you* were any kind of athlete," Pam shot back, "you would have run anyway. Or walked. Or gimped. Or whatever it is that you do on crutches, Fayne."

"Well . . ." George started to say, but she closed her mouth.

"Well, what?"

George crossed the room and sat on Pam's bed. "Well, I really missed you, Pam."

Pam leaned forward, and they wrapped each other in a tight hug.

"I'm sorry for accusing you," George said.

Pam shook her head. "No, *I'm* sorry for hurting your foot," she insisted.

"No, *I'm* sorry."

"No, *me!*"

George shrugged and smiled. "Okay!"

Pam frowned and slapped at her playfully.

"But just for the record," George explained, "what I said about your doing it on purpose, I said because I was angry at myself."

Pam lowered her eyes. "I know, but it still hurt."

George held out her hand. "Friends?"

Pam shook. "Friends."

George blew a relieved sigh as she felt a weight fall from her shoulders. "College is hard enough without being mad at your roommate," she said.

That afternoon Dawn didn't realize how tired and weak she was until she had to walk all the way from the off-campus REACH house to Thayer Hall. It was only a little over a mile, but by the time she hit the campus quad, she was breathing hard and sweating and having the shivers. Something else surprised her, too: how happy everyone on the quad looked. People were laughing, tossing Frisbees, reading under trees. People were having fun! Everyone in the REACH house was too busy studying to have any fun. "Too busy making Mitch money," she muttered bitterly.

It was as though a veil had been lifted from her eyes all at once.

Dawn was nearly faint by the time she reached the suite and crossed the lounge.

"Dawn!" Reva cried. She was standing in the hallway, wrapped in towels, fresh from the shower. "It's great to see you. Are you okay? You look kind of—"

"Sick," Dawn said, smiling feebly. "I know. Do you have anything to eat?"

"I have just the thing," Reva said, and disappeared into her room. She returned with a box of toaster pastries.

Dawn's eyes widened. "Strawberry, my favorite," she said.

Suddenly Nancy appeared in her doorway. Tears blurred Dawn's eyes. "Oh, Nancy!"

Nancy ran over and gave Dawn a hug—a *real* hug, Dawn realized. A hug that actually meant something.

Nancy put her arm around Dawn's shoulders and led Dawn into her room. Stephanie was already there, her feet on Kara's bed, plowing through the third bag of Kara's stash of nacho chips.

"Well, well, look what the cat brought in," she said dryly between mouthfuls. "We were just talking about you."

Dawn smiled weakly. "Thanks for trying to rescue me."

Stephanie shrugged. "It's that Mitch guy who

really burns me up. All that poor-talk doesn't fool me."

"No kidding," Dawn said. She looked at Nancy. "Nancy, I was so stupid. I just saw his personal bank statement."

"That's why you left?" Nancy asked.

Dawn nodded and hid her face in her hands. "He has so much money, you guys! He's squirreling it away in a separate account under his name. Oh, it's so humiliating! I can't believe I didn't see any of it. I'm so blind!"

"You were hurting," Nancy said tenderly. "You were looking for something to make you feel better."

"*Someone* is more like it," Dawn said. "I was lonely. When Peter broke up with me, I guess it was more than I could handle. But it wasn't Mitch Lebo I needed, that's for sure. Some R.A. I've been—someone to really look up to, huh?"

"You could say that again," Stephanie muttered under her breath.

"Stephanie!" Nancy said.

"Just kidding," Stephanie said. "But there's one thing I don't understand. How does Mitch get everyone to give up all their money? I mean, *I* never gave anything. No offense or anything, but is a requirement to get into REACH that you be a total idiot?"

"Stephanie!" Nancy chided her again.

Sighing, Dawn shook her head from side to side. "No, she's right. I can't believe I signed that thing."

"Signed what?" Nancy asked.

"The other night, I was so tired, I didn't know what I was doing. Mitch had me sign a contract. I don't remember everything it said, but I remember one thing. I had to give him things."

"Money?" Stephanie prodded her.

Dawn nodded. "And all my personal property," she said.

"He made you sign that?" Nancy asked in disbelief. "Boy, *that's* bold."

"I just wish I could get my money back," Dawn said. "I must have given him a couple of hundred dollars. Or even just file a complaint. Anything to get him off campus and away from everyone."

"Maybe we could take everyone in the REACH house to show them Mitch's mansion and that new car of his," Stephanie suggested.

"Forget it," Dawn said. "If you think I was tough to convince . . ."

Dawn noticed that Nancy seemed lost in thought. "What?"

"I just wonder," Nancy began. "I bet that if we could get our hands on a copy of that contract, we could get the university to do something about old Mitch Lebo and the REACHettes. Maybe even go to the police."

"But I don't have a copy," Dawn lamented.

Nancy, eyes blazing, turned her gaze on Stephanie. "But we could get it."

Stephanie held up her hands in mock surrender. "Whoa there! Not me again. I'm tired of playing house with those freaks."

"But you *and* Dawn!" Nancy said. "I'd go,

but Mitch already knows I'm bad news. But you could say you're back for one more try. Maybe you could somehow persuade him that you're really interested?"

Stephanie pursed her lips, thinking. "Boy, I just hate it when someone swindles people out of money," she said, narrowing her eyes.

For the first time in what felt like years, Dawn beamed. "That's the spirit, Steph," she said.

Stephanie eyed Dawn up and down. "But first, we have to get this girl some serious food, not those dumb pastries, and a change of clothes."

CHAPTER 13

Stephanie was actually overjoyed that Mitch was at the REACH house when she and Dawn walked through the door later that night. She wanted to see the little toad one more time and feel the pleasure of getting the evidence to put him away, right under his nose.

And just in case she had any trouble, she'd worn her white bodysuit and a pair of her tightest jeans. If a little talking couldn't do the job, some not-so-subtle bodily persuasion never failed her.

"Stephanie," Mitch said as he came out of his office to greet them. "You're always coming and going. I was beginning to wonder about you."

"Well, Mr. Lebo—"

"Mitch," Mitch said. "Always Mitch."

"Mitch," Stephanie replied, flashing her sliest and flirtiest grin. She had to hand it to him: as sleazy as he was, he was a talented guy. His act was smooth as silk.

"Dawn came back to get me," Stephanie said quickly, gazing at the silent young woman beside her. "I agreed that I hadn't really reached my potential here."

"I was wondering where you'd gone, Dawn," Mitch said, turning to her. "For a little while there, I was afraid—"

"Oh, no!" Dawn interrupted. "I felt Stephanie calling for help. I heard her in my soul."

Stephanie gritted her teeth. Lay it on *too* thick, why don't you, she thought to herself.

Mitch looked at Dawn sternly. "But in the future, don't leave the house without telling someone. Understood?"

Stephanie thought that Dawn looked ready to break, like a fragile piece of glass.

"But, Mitch," she said, stepping between them. Lifting her arms, she ran her fingers through her hair, turning her head to display her long neck. "I was also thinking that I could really help the group. You know, help it get what it needs."

Stephanie didn't miss the flicker in Mitch's eye. "What do you mean?" he asked.

Stephanie shrugged and looked away coyly, trying to seem shy. "Well, my daddy's kind of got a lot of money, and he gives me a nice allowance every semester. I just thought I could help with a little something."

Mitch was nodding, his expression suddenly more friendly. "Good, Stephanie. That's a good start."

"But I didn't just come back with money," Stephanie went on. "I have some questions."

"All right," Mitch said reluctantly, throwing an impatient glance at Dawn.

"I'll go study," Dawn said, moving off.

Out of the corner of her eye, Stephanie could see her heading for Mitch's office.

"So," she said, leading Mitch away by the hand.

But he took his hand back and put it safely in his pocket. "You had questions?" he asked matter-of-factly.

Impossibly, he wasn't responding at all. Stephanie decided to try the listen 'n' learn method.

"I was wondering where you were from," she said, leaning back against the wall, the better to display herself.

"Where I'm from is of no consequence," Mitch began. "And you know, Stephanie, you don't need to resort to flirting to get the attention that will make you happy."

Stephanie's face froze. The nerve!

"Be happy in another way," Mitch continued. "Like giving of yourself to REACH, for instance."

"Really," Stephanie said, using every ounce of energy to fake her interest. "Tell me more."

Inside, though, she was boiling over.

What a double-crossing phony, she seethed. And where does the little creep come off telling me not to be sexy!

Luckily, Dawn returned just as she was about to say something she knew she'd regret.

169

"Stephanie, I can't believe I forgot my clothes!" she said, tapping her temple. "What a dummy."

"But you have *everything else,* don't you?" Stephanie asked meaningfully.

Dawn nodded. "We'll be back in a half hour, Mitch. I just have to get the rest of my things."

"But we have a group session starting in about five minutes," he said, eyeing them suspiciously.

Dawn sidled up to his side. "But I don't want to have to go back there again ever," she said, sniffing. "After tonight, my decision is complete."

"You're dropping out of Wilder?" Mitch asked.

Dawn nodded. "First thing in the morning."

Mitch nodded. "I'll wait until you get back to tell the others. You're a model for us all, Dawn."

Once Stephanie and she were outside, Dawn slipped a piece of paper out of her pocket, unfolded it, and clutched it. "Got it!" she cried.

Stephanie patted her on the back. "Academy Award–winning performance," she said. "You even made *me* proud."

Practically deserted, Java Joe's was about to close for the night. The only people left were the counter staff and an exhausted student who'd fallen asleep in a booth, clutching a cup of coffee.

Paul checked his watch for the fiftieth time. He was already on his third cup of cappuccino, with enough caffeine in him to fuel a personal space-shot to the moon.

She didn't like the date book, Paul told himself

dejectedly. I have to admit, it was a pretty silly idea. I mean, I know Brian thought it was funny and that it would work, but Bess is probably too sophisticated. I should have done something more savvy. Maybe tickets to a concert or something.

Suddenly, like a nightmare, the picture of himself singing up at Bess's window played in his mind for the hundredth time. He winced.

That was *so* cornball, he reprimanded himself. She's definitely not going to show. She probably thinks you're a total fool. Stretching, he closed one eye and stole a peek at his watch.

"Two minutes late," he murmured. "She absolutely thinks I'm a dork. I don't have a chance."

He rose to go. But the door opened, and a beautiful blonde was standing in the doorway. She had sparkling blue eyes and a mouth on the verge of a permanent smile.

She walked slowly around the tables, twisting her way toward him. Paul lowered himself to the bench, his only thought: Wow.

"You know, ten minutes doesn't give a girl much time to arrive fashionably late," she said.

Paul smiled up at Bess. I *know* this is going to work, he told himself. It's going to be something *really* good.

"This is good," Nancy said, poring over the REACH contract at her desk. "This is *really* good."

"Did we nail him?" Dawn asked.

Nancy turned and smiled at Dawn. *"You* nailed him," she said.

"Boy, Dawn really scared me," Stephanie said. "She was so good back there, she had me convinced she'd gone back to REACH forever. You should have seen her sniff! What a heartbreaker. But you know what this means, don't you?"

Dawn smiled at her. "What?"

"It means that from now on, I know just how well you can lie. And that means, you can't get away with anything, not with me."

"No problem," Dawn replied. "But I still feel like an idiot. How's the contract looking, Nancy?"

"Well, to be honest, it's bad, but I don't see anything illegal. Maybe enough to get him kicked off campus, but not enough to have him put behind bars. Wait, wait a second!"

Nancy planted her finger on the very bottom of the last page. "Here's the clause you were talking about, Dawn. It says, 'Every member will support the group by giving all their material possessions.' "

Dawn hid her head in Kara's pillows. "I can't *believe* I signed that!"

Stephanie whistled. "Me neither."

"I was so tired—" Dawn said.

"Unfortunately," Nancy said, "there's nothing illegal with this, either. Unless, wait." Nancy blinked. She looked at Dawn. "What did you just say?"

"What?" Dawn asked.

"About being tired."

Dawn shrugged. "I don't know. It was weird. I was so hungry. And all night they were giving me that drink, telling me it was good for me. And then those pills. I was so groggy. Then Mitch comes in and asks me to sign."

"That's it!" Nancy blurted out. "That's it, that's what we need! That's why he starved you and kept you up studying so many nights in a row. He doped you, Dawn! And that, unfortunately for them, is very illegal!"

"You bet it is," Stephanie chimed in. "Is Mitch's signature on that contract?"

Nancy nodded. "Yes, it's official." She thumbed toward the door. "And he's officially going to be out of here!"

Kara and Tim were walking hand in hand through the pools of lamplight crisscrossing the campus quad. Though it was late at night, it wasn't too cold, and the moon shadows under each tree were occupied by circles of students.

"Isn't college great?" Kara said. "I mean, look at this place. It's the most peaceful, fun place on earth."

Tim squeezed Kara's hand. "You're so enthusiastic all the time," he said.

"But that's why you like me so much," Kara said.

Tim laughed. "Are you asking or telling?"

"Both."

Tim nodded. "Then you're right, that's why I like you so much."

They turned and circled back past the Student

Union. In the windows, they could see people playing pool in the game room.

Suddenly Kara froze. She pointed up at the window, where a girl was bent over a pool table, lining up a shot.

"Hey, that's my vest! My favorite leather vest!"

Tim squinted through the window. "What?"

"That girl! That's the vest I lent Montana for the postrace party at Pi Phi."

"Do you know that girl?"

Kara slapped her forehead. "I can't believe it. No, I *don't* know that girl!"

Tim scratched his head. "Then why is she wearing it?"

"That's the problem! Oh, I knew this would happen. It's my worst nightmare!"

Tim shook his head. "Would you please tell me what's going on?"

Kara looked up at Tim and was about to tell him everything: Montana and Nikki and their clothes, and *her* clothes, and trading the bracelet for a dance with him, and the rest of it.

But she didn't.

"It's too complicated," she fumed. "Men just wouldn't understand."

CHAPTER 14

Dawn burst excitedly through the door to Suite 301, towing Bill Graham behind her. It felt great to be back in the dorm and in her own life.

"Hey, just the person I wanted to see," Dawn said as she saw Nancy coming out of her room.

"Dawn, Bill, what's up?" Nancy asked as she came into the lounge, a bag of books slung over her shoulder.

"I just wanted to let you know what happened with the REACH stuff." Dawn was smiling. "First of all, I stopped by the house, and everyone was really upset because Mitch hadn't shown up yet."

"He took off," Bill added, his grin almost splitting his face. "Closed his personal account and vanished."

"Too bad we won't get the money back," Dawn replied. "But at least he's gone. And just in case, I gave a copy of that contract I signed and a statement to the university. They said they'd turn it over to the D.A.'s office. I told them about the doping, and they thought they'd be able to charge him."

Dawn sighed. "No more REACH posters or leaflets." She thought of all the kids who were still lingering around the house. "It's so sad, though. There are a lot of people who are still really hung up on him."

"What will happen to them?" Nancy asked.

"Someone in the dean's office mentioned something about setting up a support network for them," Dawn said, waving a hand. "You know, with school psychologists or something."

"You sound so skeptical," Nancy replied. "Don't you think it will help?"

Dawn nodded. "Yes, but they'll need someone with experience, someone who's been there. I thought I'd volunteer for a while. It has to be done right. I mean, *I* didn't even believe it when you guys told me the truth. If I hadn't seen those deposit slips myself . . ." Dawn trailed off.

She was suddenly imagining what might have happened if she hadn't seen for herself how she was being duped. She shuddered and felt Bill put his arm around her and give her a quick hug.

"But you did," he said. "Don't think about it anymore. Remember the plan for tonight."

"That's right." Dawn laughed, suddenly brightening. "Spend money! On myself! Shop till I drop!"

Bill leaned over to Nancy.

"She's really bummed now about missing that concert," he whispered loudly. "I'm going to rub it in for weeks. Hum the songs."

"Bill!" Nancy cried, snatching at his arm. "You're awful. Don't listen to him."

Dawn grabbed Bill by the arm. "He'll talk about the concert I missed, but he won't tell you how hard it was to get him to go to the movies with me."

She looked up at Bill. He groaned and held his heart. All of a sudden, Dawn felt a funny skip in her own heart. She was really looking forward to going out and celebrating her freedom again, and if she'd had to pick one person to join her, she couldn't think of anyone better than Bill. He always knew how to put her in a good mood.

"I don't know," Dawn replied mysteriously. "I feel like I just opened my eyes or something. All around me familiar things are looking new." She grinned up at Bill. "Like I never really saw them before."

Dawn saw Nancy and Bill exchange glances, and she didn't miss the wink Nancy sent him either.

"And what's that for?" Dawn asked. "Don't forget I'm still the R.A. here," she teased threateningly. "Keeping secrets with another R.A. is like mutiny. I might have to toss you out of my suite."

"Don't worry," Nancy replied with a twinkle in her eye. "I'm sure you'll figure it out yourself before too long. And if you don't, just ask Bill. He'll tell you."

"W-well, uh," Bill stammered, and his face turned bright red. Dawn almost felt like laughing. He was really so funny and sweet. She hooked her arm through his and grinned.

"Bill knows," she murmured. "Well, Mr. Graham, we have ways of making you talk."

"Oh, I'm sure you do," Bill said with a gulp.

"Come on then." Dawn gave his arm a tug. "The movie will distract you, and then I'll ply you with food and drink. If you've got a secret, I'll know it by the end of the night."

"I hope you will," Bill said happily.

"You look awfully cheerful for an invalid," Will joked as George hobbled into the living room of his apartment. "Anything happen today that I might be interested in?"

"As a matter of fact, yes," George admitted happily, swinging herself over to the couch and collapsing onto Will's stomach.

"Oomph," he cried, as he lifted George into a more comfortable position. "No need to break my ribs about it. I'll listen."

"Well," George said, "I went by my room today."

"*Your* room?" Will furrowed his brow. "You have a *room* somewhere?"

"Okay, okay." George laughed. "So maybe I

was hiding out here. Anyway, I did go back to *my* room. And"—George grinned—"I saw Pam."

"And?" Will prodded.

"We talked everything out and made up. It was just a huge misunderstanding, and I'm so glad we spoke to each other," George said in a rush. Then she put her fingers against Will's lips. "*And* thank you for being such a good sport while I was sulking. And for saying 'I told you so' and for telling me to talk to her, because of course you were right."

"So you two are friends again, right?" Will asked relieved.

"Right," George agreed. "So how was your day?"

"Pretty good." Will grinned, his own eyes filling with excitement. "I was on the phone all day again today. I finally got to the right people."

"And?" George asked excitedly.

"They've agreed to lend me the Cherokee art pieces, if my proposal for the show is the one selected."

"Oh, Will!" George threw her arms around his neck. "That's fantastic."

"Hold on, hold on," Will choked out. "None of this means I get the show. I still have to submit my proposal."

"But this is such an excellent idea for that new art series," George replied. "Of course you'll get it."

"I'm glad you think so." Will smiled. "You're like my own personal cheerleading squad." He grabbed her and gave her a tight squeeze.

"Wait, have mercy," George cried playfully. "I'm still an invalid." She leaned over and snuggled against Will's shoulder. "Which means that you'll still be nice to me and rub my back and bring me treats, won't you?"

"I'll answer your question if you answer a question of mine," he said seductively.

"Just ask," George said.

"Exactly *how* much of an invalid are you still? Is that *invalid* as in totally and completely bedridden?"

George felt a pleasant tickle begin in the pit of her stomach as she stared into Will's eyes.

"I'd say most certainly definitely bedridden," she murmured.

"That's good," Will grinned wickedly. "Then the answer to your question is that I'll most certainly definitely be nice to you."

"Hmmmm." George sighed, leaning against his chest.

"*And* I'll bring you all kinds of treats." His breath was like a feather against her lips.

"Hmmmm," George agreed as she leaned in to deepen the kiss. "I *love* treats."

As Nancy neared Jake's apartment house, her footsteps became quieter. The streetlight was out; so were the house lamps. Most of the windows were dark. It was late, but it was also Thursday night, a big night for music at the Underground, the campus club for alternative music. A lot of people in Jake's apartment house were probably there.

As Nancy approached, she thought she saw the old loveseat in the corner of the old-fashioned front porch move. She heard a creak.

"Is anybody there?" she called.

There was a pause, then Jake's voice filled the space. "It depends."

Nancy smiled to herself. "Depends on what?"

"On whether whoever is still mad."

"What if she was?"

"Then no one's here," he said.

Nancy thought about the miscommunication with Jake over her promotion. After the meeting at the newspaper the day before, when it was clear from what Gail had said that she was the only one who had made the decision to give Nancy the promotion, Nancy realized she owed Jake an apology. Nancy had gotten the promotion because Gail thought she deserved it. Jake had known that all along.

"I'm not mad," she said.

"Then someone's here," he called back. "Want to come up?"

"I was hoping you'd ask."

Nancy climbed the steps and sat on the loveseat. She could feel Jake beside her in the dark, breathing deeply. "You know," she began, "all my life, everything I've ever done has always been my choice. And every success has been on my own terms."

"That's one of the things I like about you so much," Jake replied. "I'd never try to undo that."

"I know that now, and I'm sorry I didn't believe that before," Nancy said. She pressed her finger to Jake's lips. "But just because I want to make a life for myself doesn't mean I'm not capable of being stubborn. I'm sorry," she said. "I let my insecurities get the best of me. I know I'm an okay writer."

"A great writer," Jake corrected her.

Nancy smiled. "Whatever. But I'm too sensitive about doing things on my own. I know that."

"You're one of the most independent people I've ever known," Jake said seriously.

"But stubborn, right?"

"I guess," Jake said quietly.

They sat for a minute in silence, listening to the sounds of the night close in on them.

Finally Nancy took a big breath. "I found out this week what happens to people who can't recognize when people care about them. I know how much you care about me, Jake. You showed me that. And maybe what scares me is how much that already means to me. It's so soon, and I've been trying to stay away from romance for a while. But I can't seem to stay away from you. I can't stop thinking about you, or wanting to be with you."

Jake swallowed hard. "Do you *want* to stop being with me?" he asked in a voice barely above a whisper.

Nancy shook her head.

"I can't tell what you did in the dark," Jake said. "Was that a yes or a no?"

"It was this," Nancy said. She felt for Jake's hand and took it in both of hers. Then she felt for his face, leaned over and kissed him passionately. It was the deepest, longest, most tender kiss Nancy had ever had.

"I guess that was a yes," Jake said after they pulled apart.

Nancy's heart was galloping. "That," she said, "was definitely a yes."

NEXT IN NANCY DREW ON CAMPUS™:

Nancy's stunning exposé in the *Wilder Times* about the cultlike group REACH is making headlines. But that's certainly not the only news on campus. The breaking story concerns Will Blackfeather, whose exhibit of Native American artifacts could turn into a disaster—if Nancy doesn't find out who's stealing the show. For Bess, the story is Paul, who sent her on a treasure hunt, in which she's bound to make some unexpected discoveries. Ginny and Ray are also looking to find something special together . . . if her parents don't stand in the way. As for Nancy, item number one is still Jake. He's taking her out to celebrate her success, and if she's willing, he'll do it with a passion . . . in *Getting Closer,* Nancy Drew on Campus #8.